DreamWo

HOME

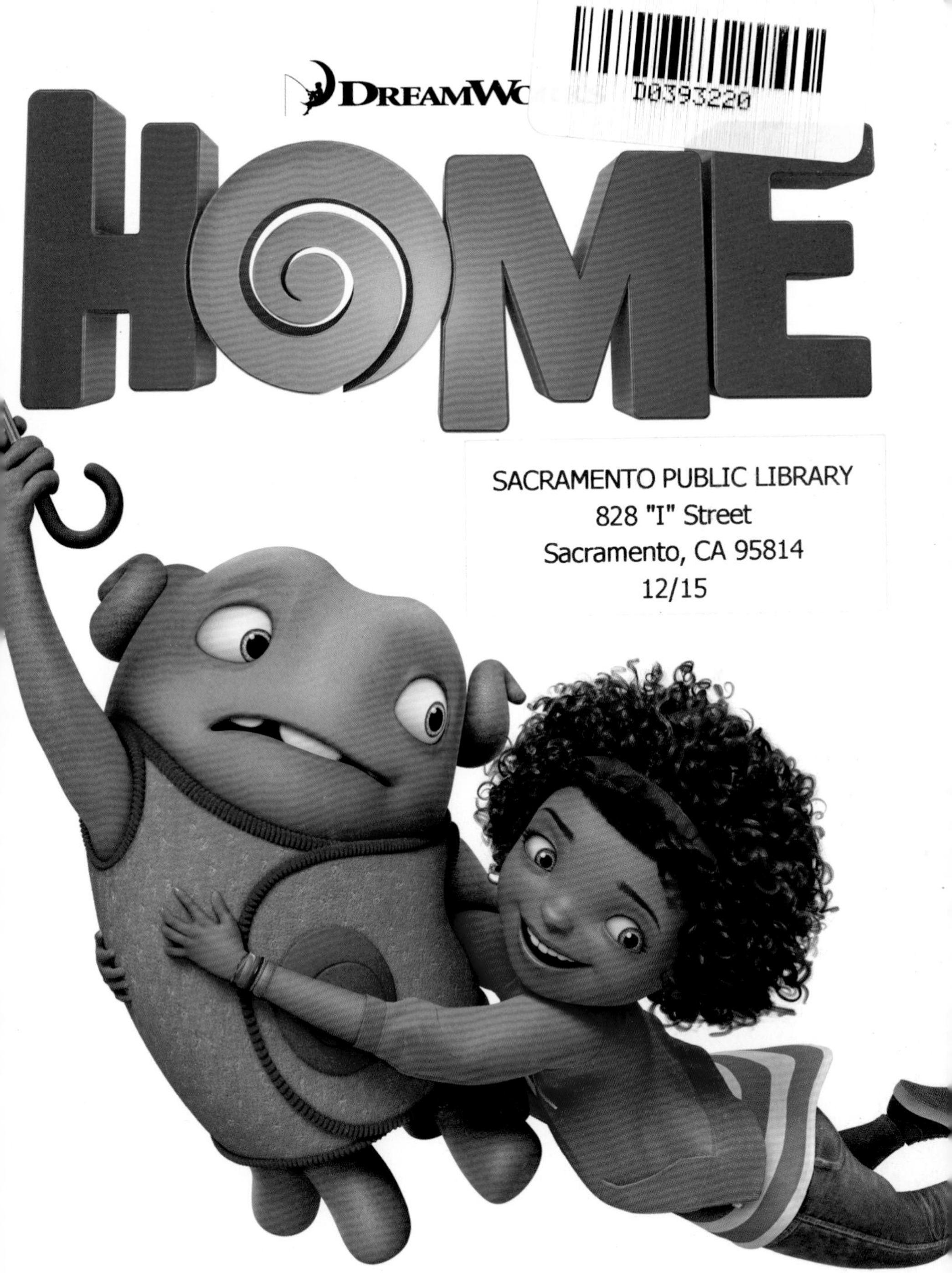

Volume Two: Another Home

DreamWorks

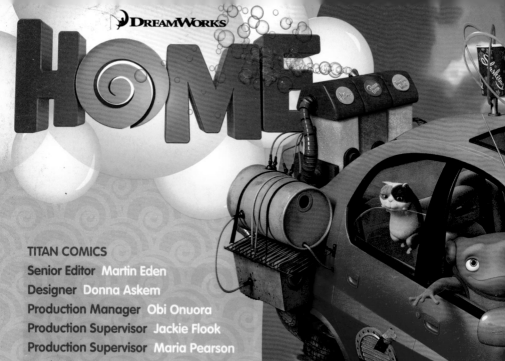

HOME

TITAN COMICS

Senior Editor Martin Eden
Designer Donna Askem
Production Manager Obi Onuora
Production Supervisor Jackie Flook
Production Supervisor Maria Pearson
Production Assistant Peter James
Studio Manager Selina Juneja
Senior Sales Manager Steve Tothill
Marketing Manager Ricky Claydon
Publishing Manager Darryl Tothill
Publishing Director Chris Teather
Operations Director Leigh Baulch
Executive Director Vivian Cheung
Publisher Nick Landau

ISBN: 9781782762294
Published by Titan Comics,
a division of Titan Publishing Group Ltd.
144 Southwark St. London, SE1 0UP

56
BOOV BAFFLER
HAVE YOU SEEN US?
Tip
Pig
Kyle
Captain Smek
ANSWERS

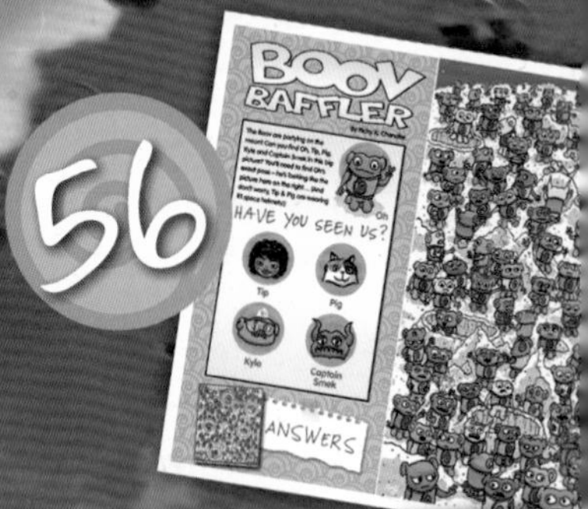

10 9 8 7 6 5 4 3 2 1
First printed in China in November 2015.
A CIP catalogue record for this title is available from the British Library.
Titan Comics. TC0534

8

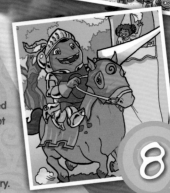

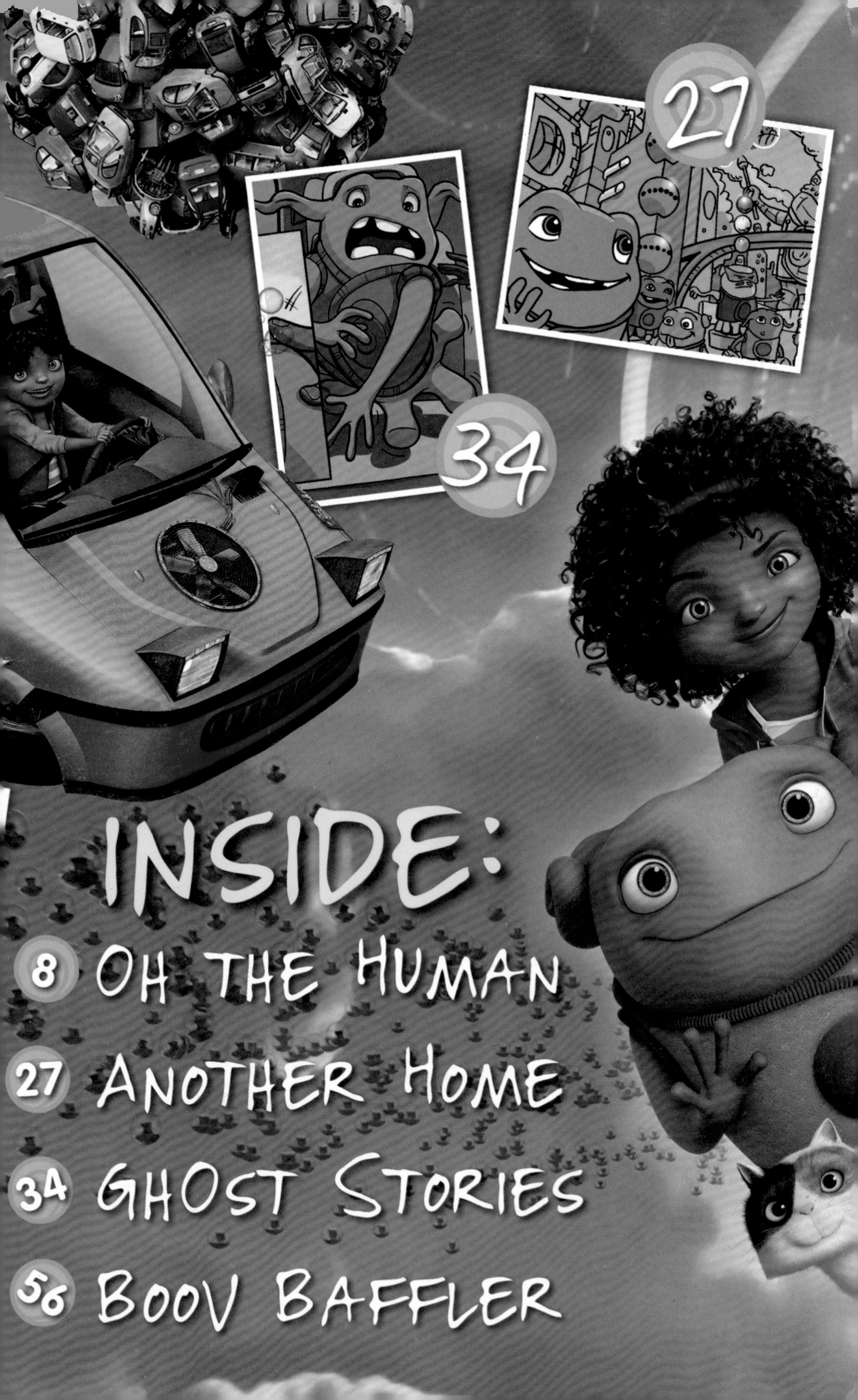
27
34

INSIDE:

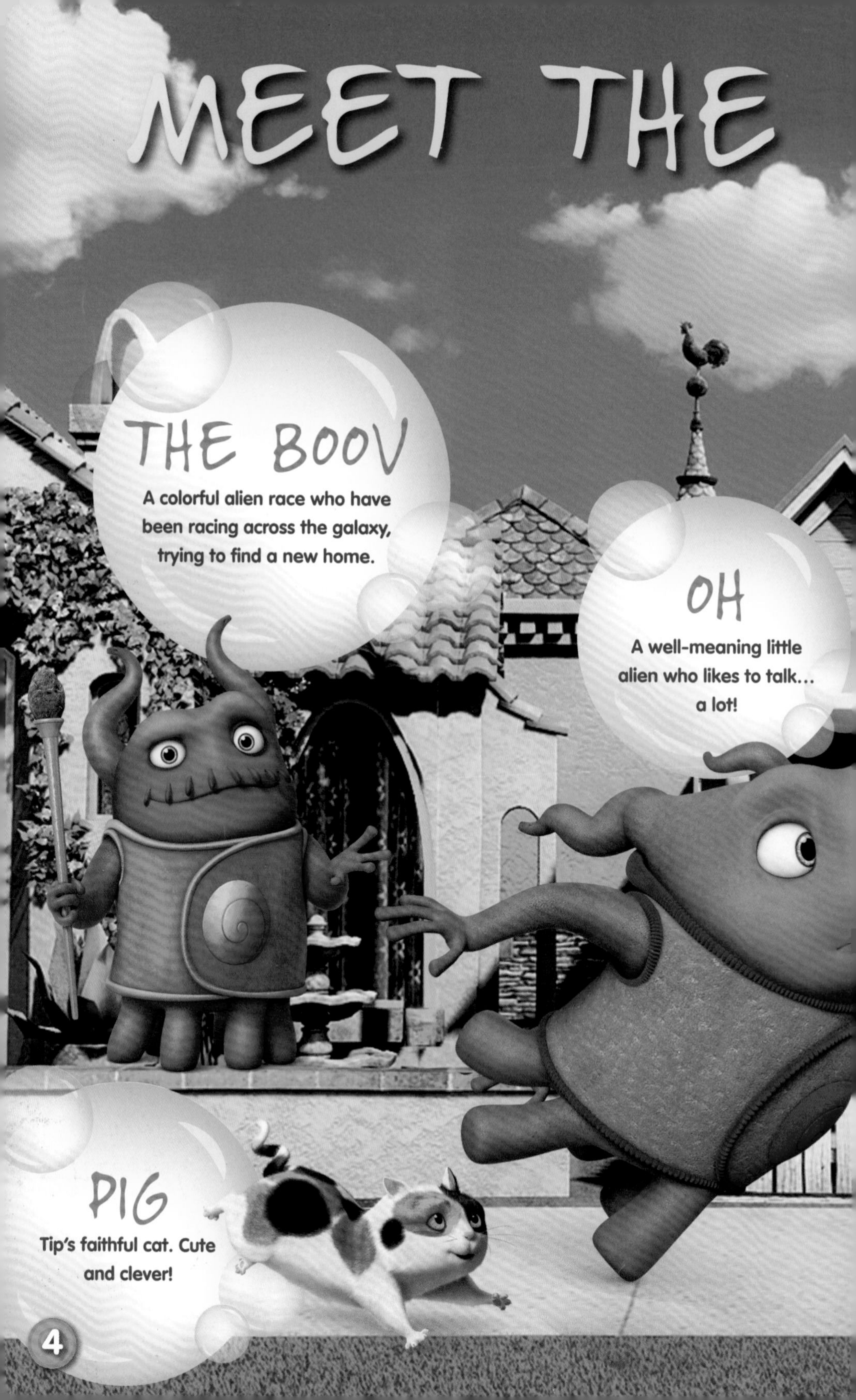

MEET THE

THE BOOV

A colorful alien race who have been racing across the galaxy, trying to find a new home.

OH

A well-meaning little alien who likes to talk… a lot!

PIG

Tip's faithful cat. Cute and clever!

HOME CREW!

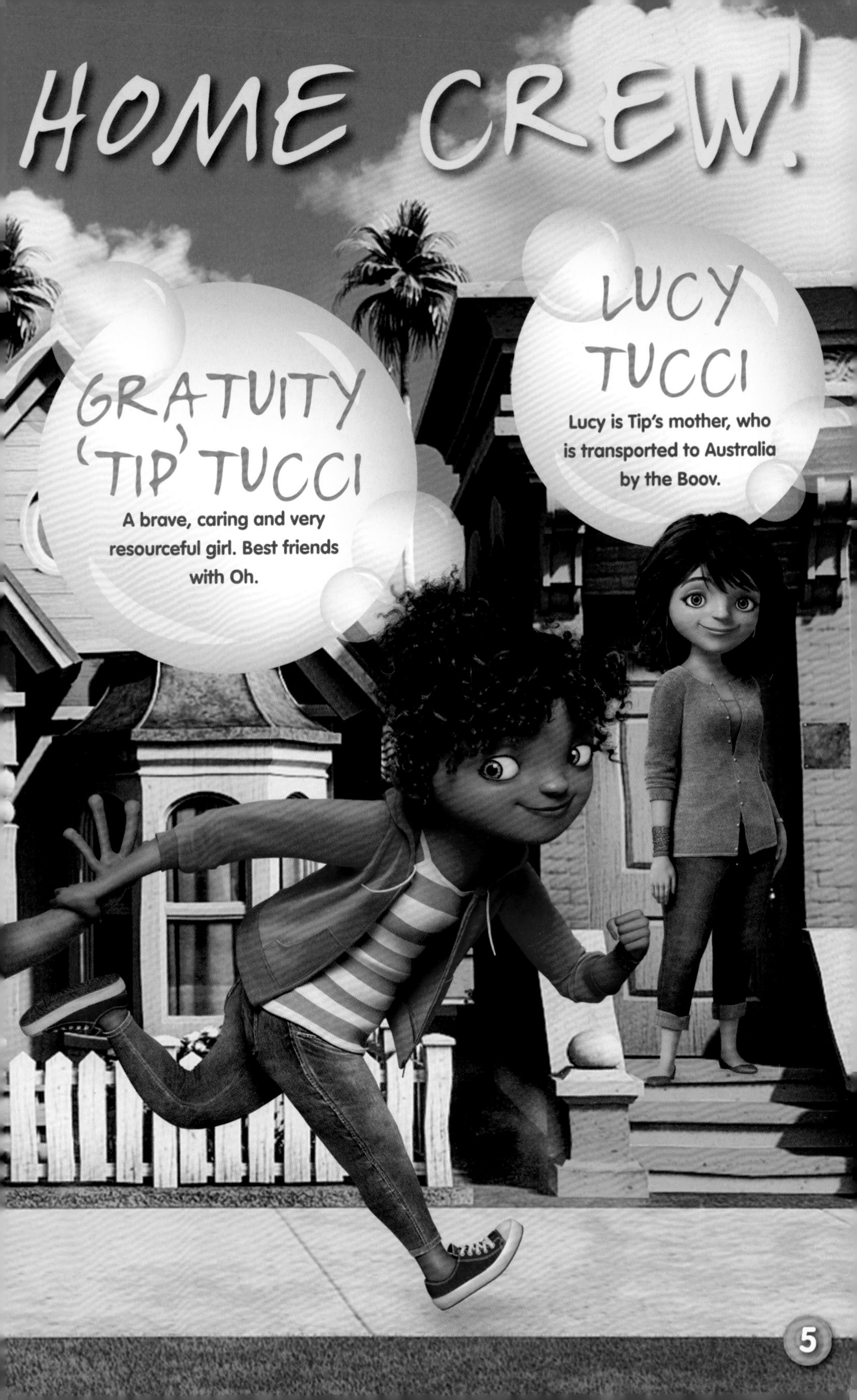

GRATUITY 'TIP' TUCCI

A brave, caring and very resourceful girl. Best friends with Oh.

LUCY TUCCI

Lucy is Tip's mother, who is transported to Australia by the Boov.

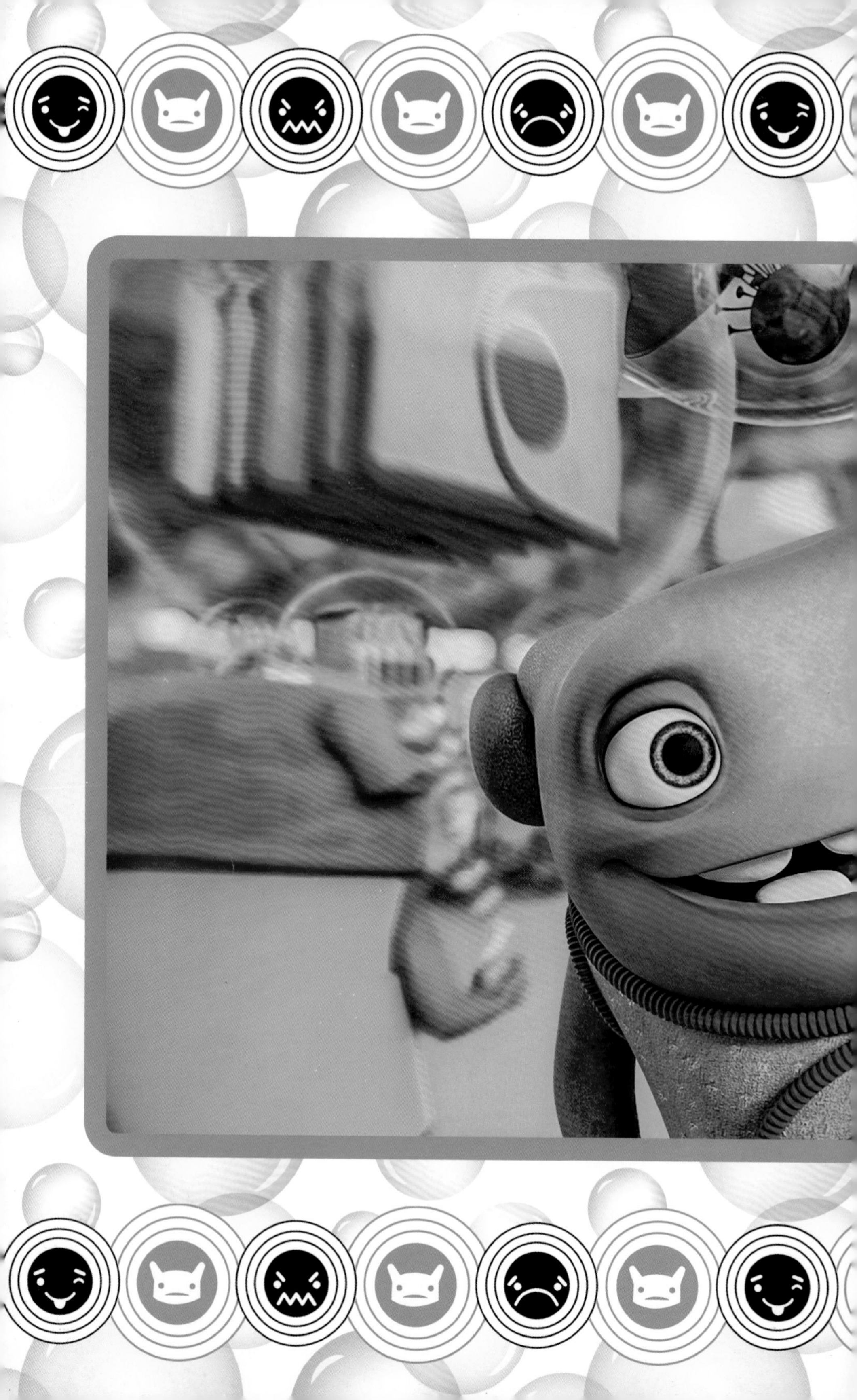

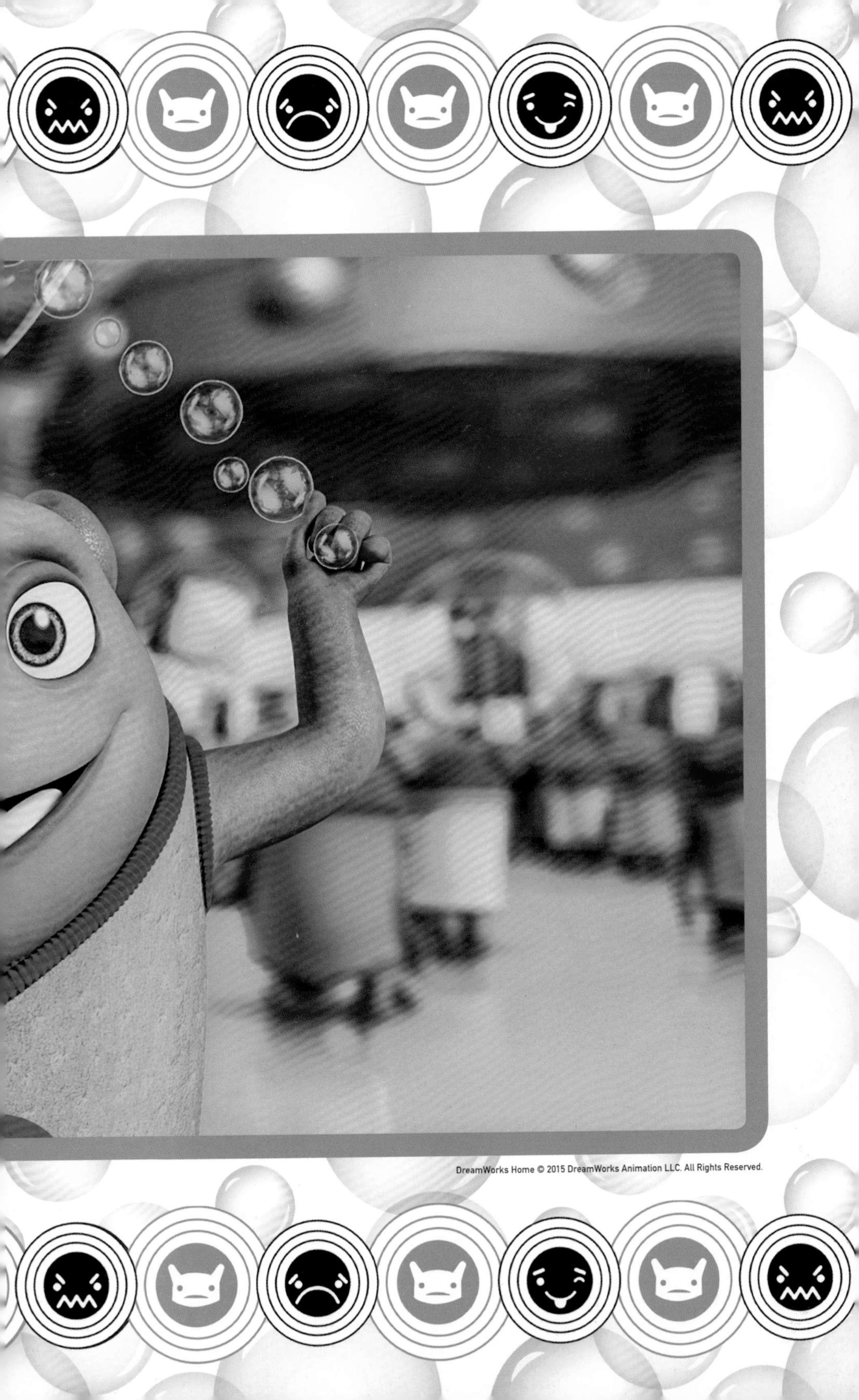

OH THE HUMAN

WRITER Max Davison
ART Alex Dalton
COLORS Phil Elliott
LETTERS Jim Campbell

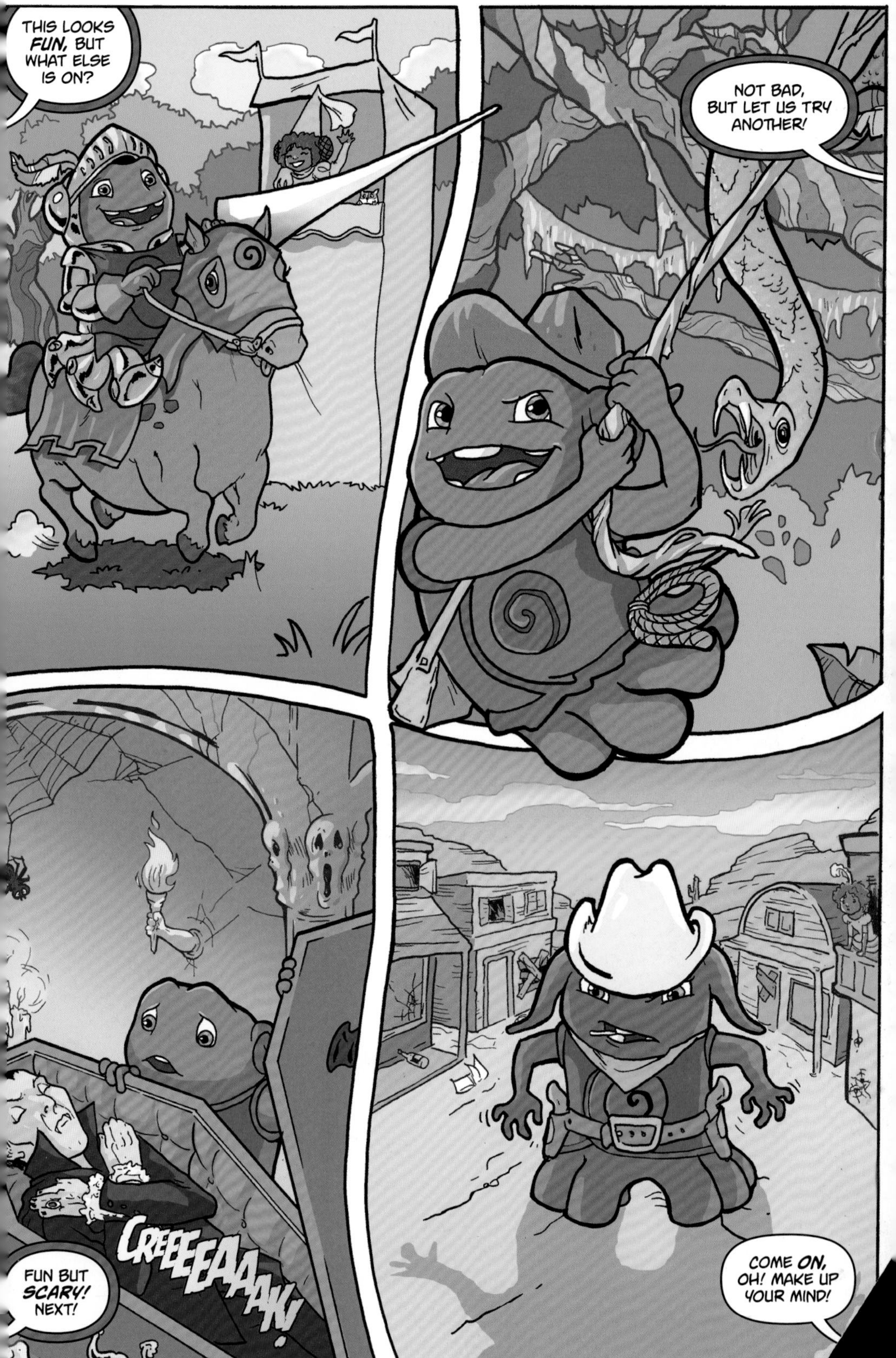
THIS LOOKS *FUN,* BUT WHAT ELSE IS ON?
NOT BAD, BUT LET US TRY ANOTHER!
CREEEEAAAAK!
FUN BUT *SCARY!* NEXT!
COME *ON,* OH! MAKE UP YOUR MIND!

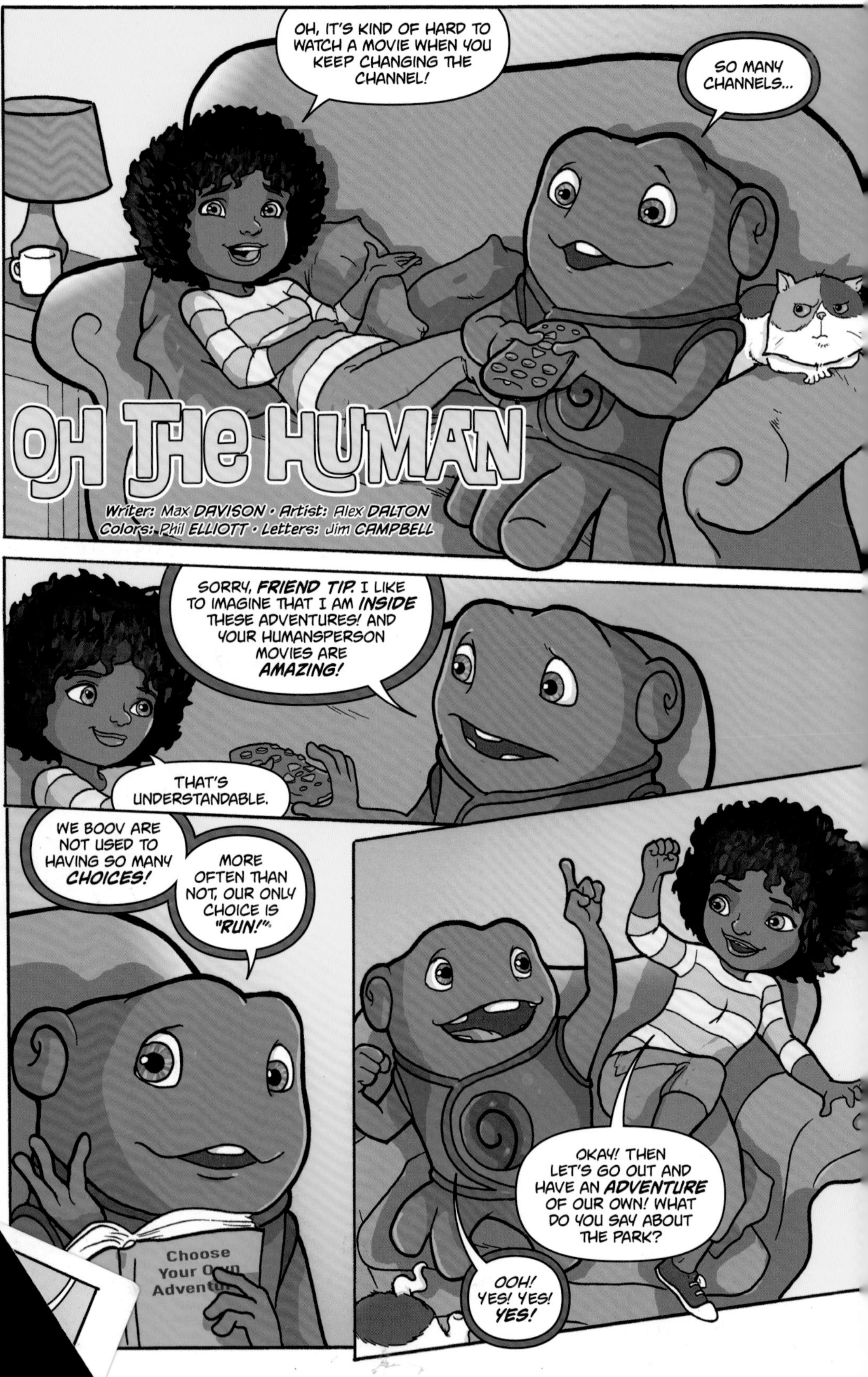
OH, IT'S KIND OF HARD TO WATCH A MOVIE WHEN YOU KEEP CHANGING THE CHANNEL!
SO MANY CHANNELS...
OH THE HUMAN
Writer: Max DAVISON • Artist: Alex DALTON
Colors: Phil ELLIOTT • Letters: Jim CAMPBELL
SORRY, FRIEND TIP. I LIKE TO IMAGINE THAT I AM INSIDE THESE ADVENTURES! AND YOUR HUMANSPERSON MOVIES ARE AMAZING!
THAT'S UNDERSTANDABLE.
WE BOOV ARE NOT USED TO HAVING SO MANY CHOICES!
MORE OFTEN THAN NOT, OUR ONLY CHOICE IS "RUN!"
Choose Your Own Adventure
OKAY! THEN LET'S GO OUT AND HAVE AN ADVENTURE OF OUR OWN! WHAT DO YOU SAY ABOUT THE PARK?
OOH! YES! YES! YES!

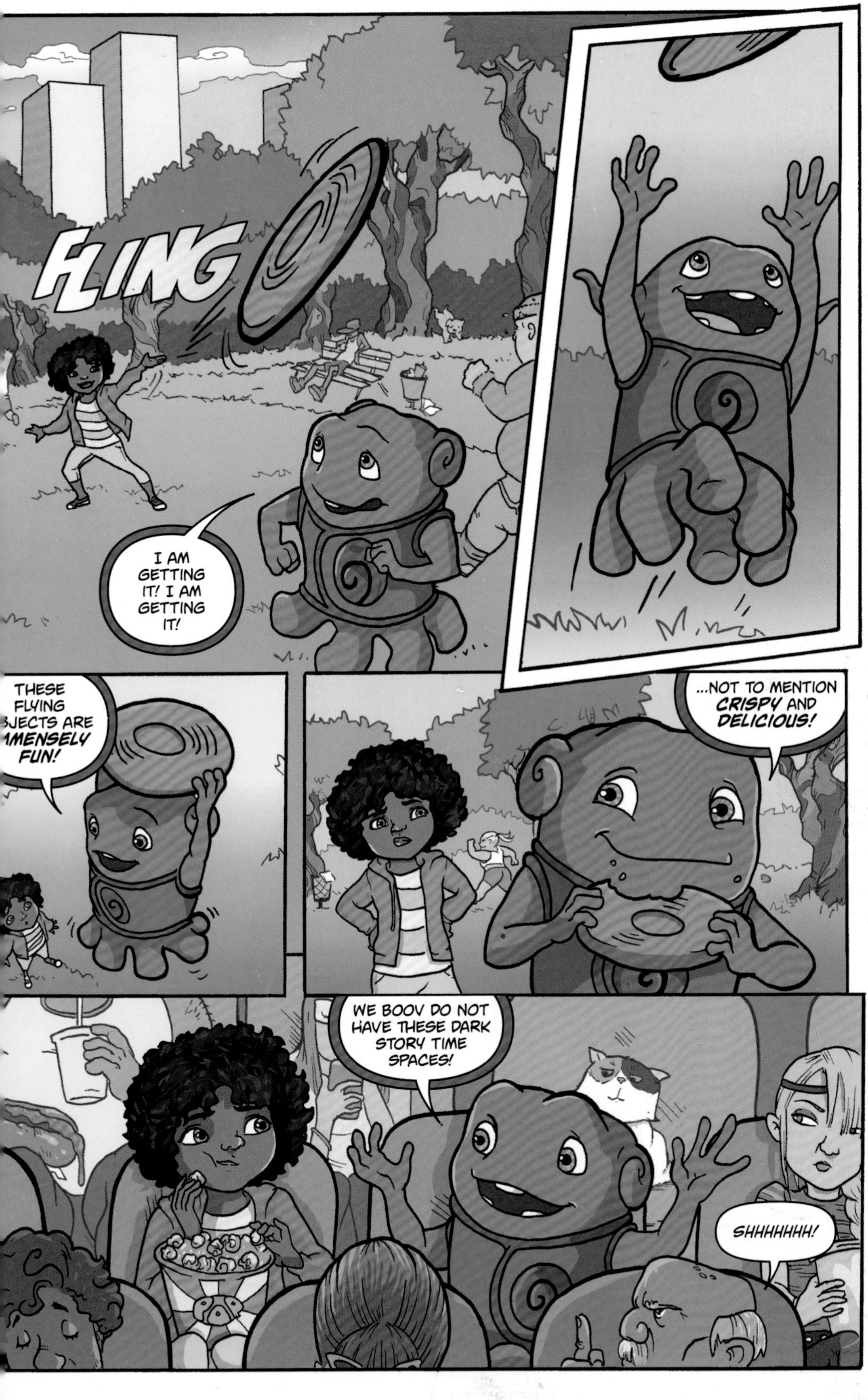
FLING
I AM GETTING IT! I AM GETTING IT!
THESE FLYING BJECTS ARE MMENSELY FUN!
...NOT TO MENTION CRISPY AND DELICIOUS!
WE BOOV DO NOT HAVE THESE DARK STORY TIME SPACES!
SHHHHHHH!

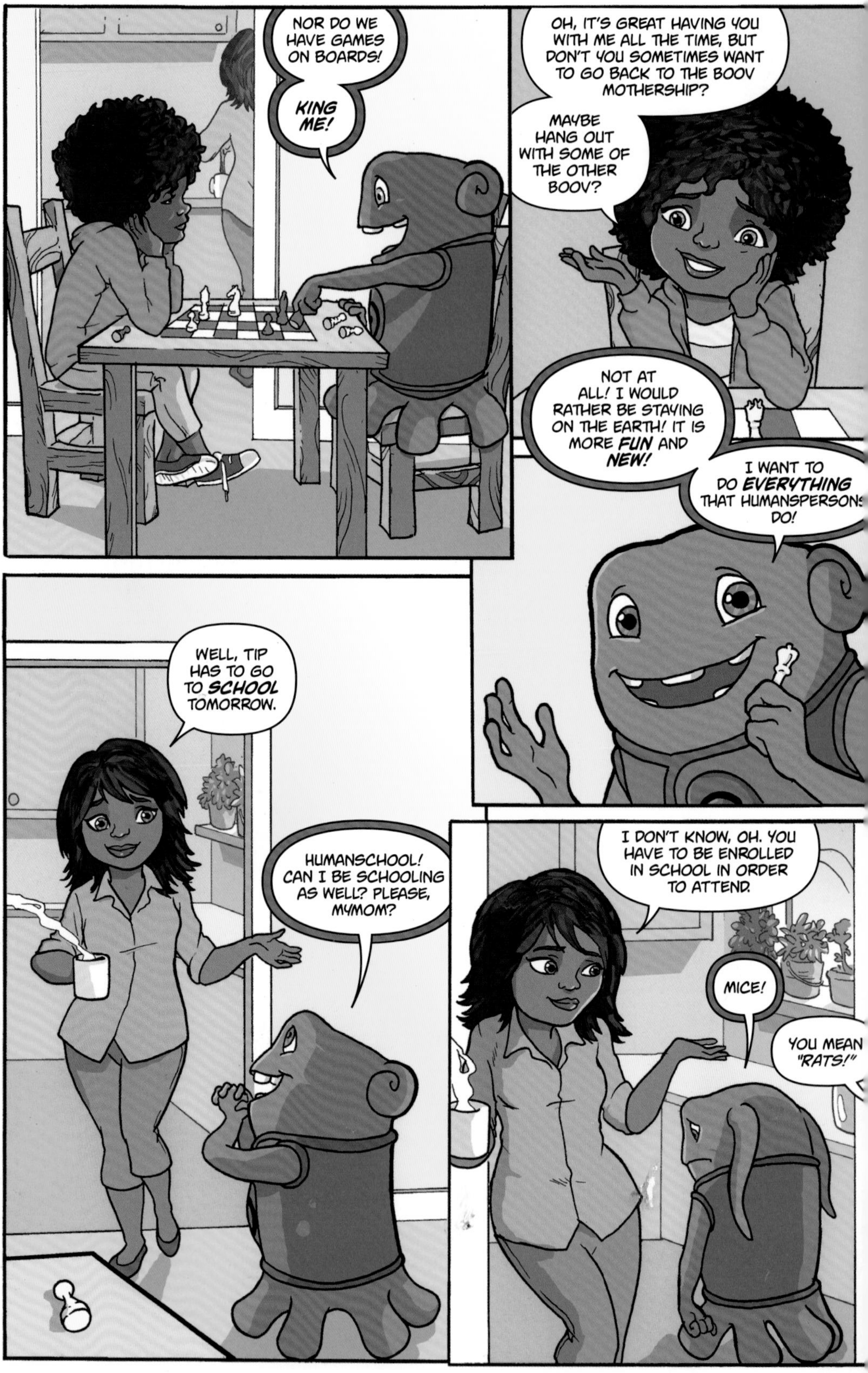
NOR DO WE HAVE GAMES ON BOARDS!
KING ME!
OH, IT'S GREAT HAVING YOU WITH ME ALL THE TIME, BUT DON'T YOU SOMETIMES WANT TO GO BACK TO THE BOOV MOTHERSHIP?
MAYBE HANG OUT WITH SOME OF THE OTHER BOOV?
NOT AT ALL! I WOULD RATHER BE STAYING ON THE EARTH! IT IS MORE FUN AND NEW!
I WANT TO DO EVERYTHING THAT HUMANSPERSONS DO!
WELL, TIP HAS TO GO TO SCHOOL TOMORROW.
HUMANSCHOOL! CAN I BE SCHOOLING AS WELL? PLEASE, MYMOM?
I DON'T KNOW, OH. YOU HAVE TO BE ENROLLED IN SCHOOL IN ORDER TO ATTEND.
MICE!
YOU MEAN "RATS!"

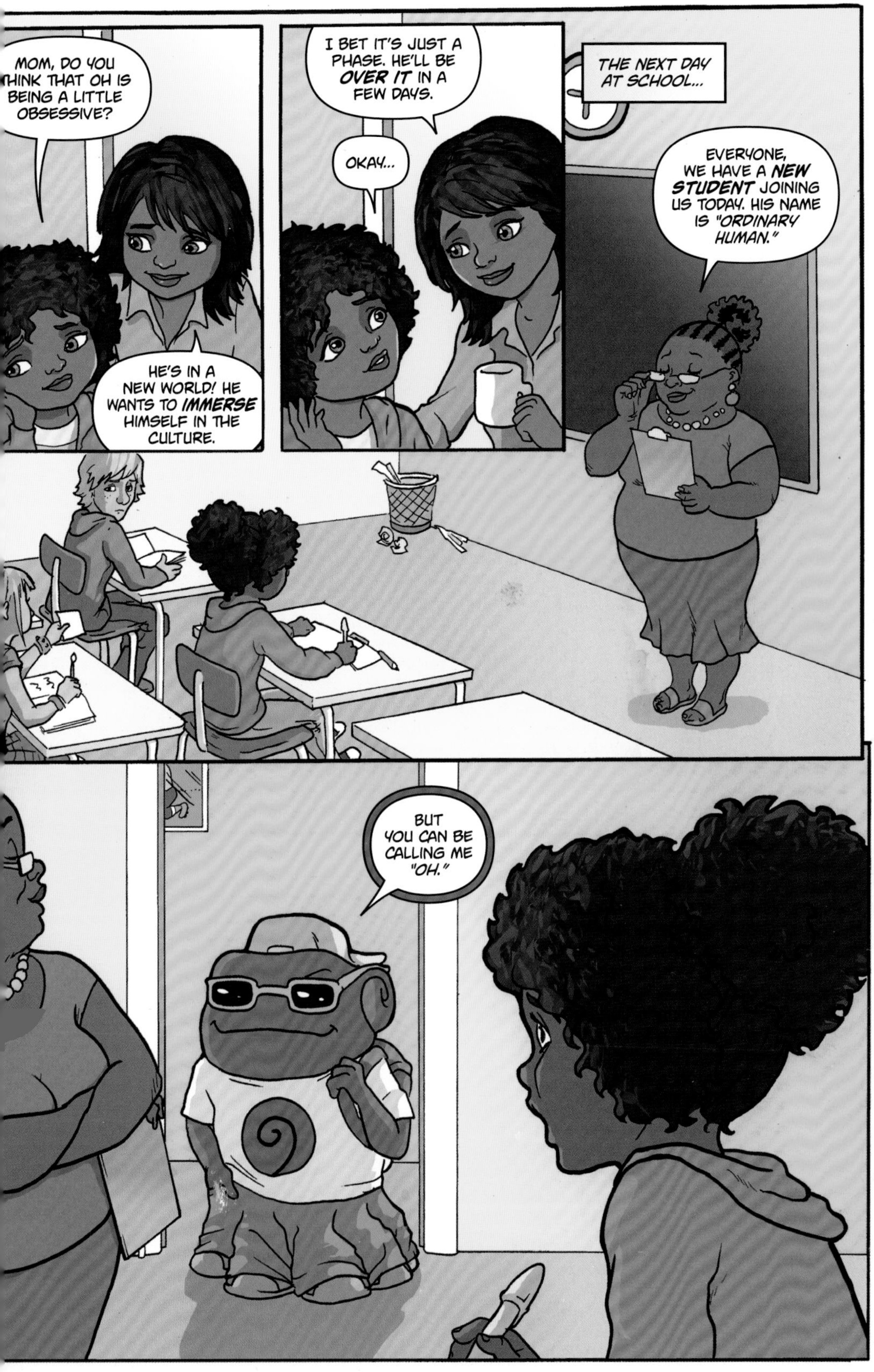
MOM, DO YOU THINK THAT OH IS BEING A LITTLE OBSESSIVE?
HE'S IN A NEW WORLD! HE WANTS TO *IMMERSE* HIMSELF IN THE CULTURE.
I BET IT'S JUST A PHASE. HE'LL BE *OVER IT* IN A FEW DAYS.
OKAY...
THE NEXT DAY AT SCHOOL...
EVERYONE, WE HAVE A *NEW STUDENT* JOINING US TODAY. HIS NAME IS "ORDINARY HUMAN."
BUT YOU CAN BE CALLING ME "OH."

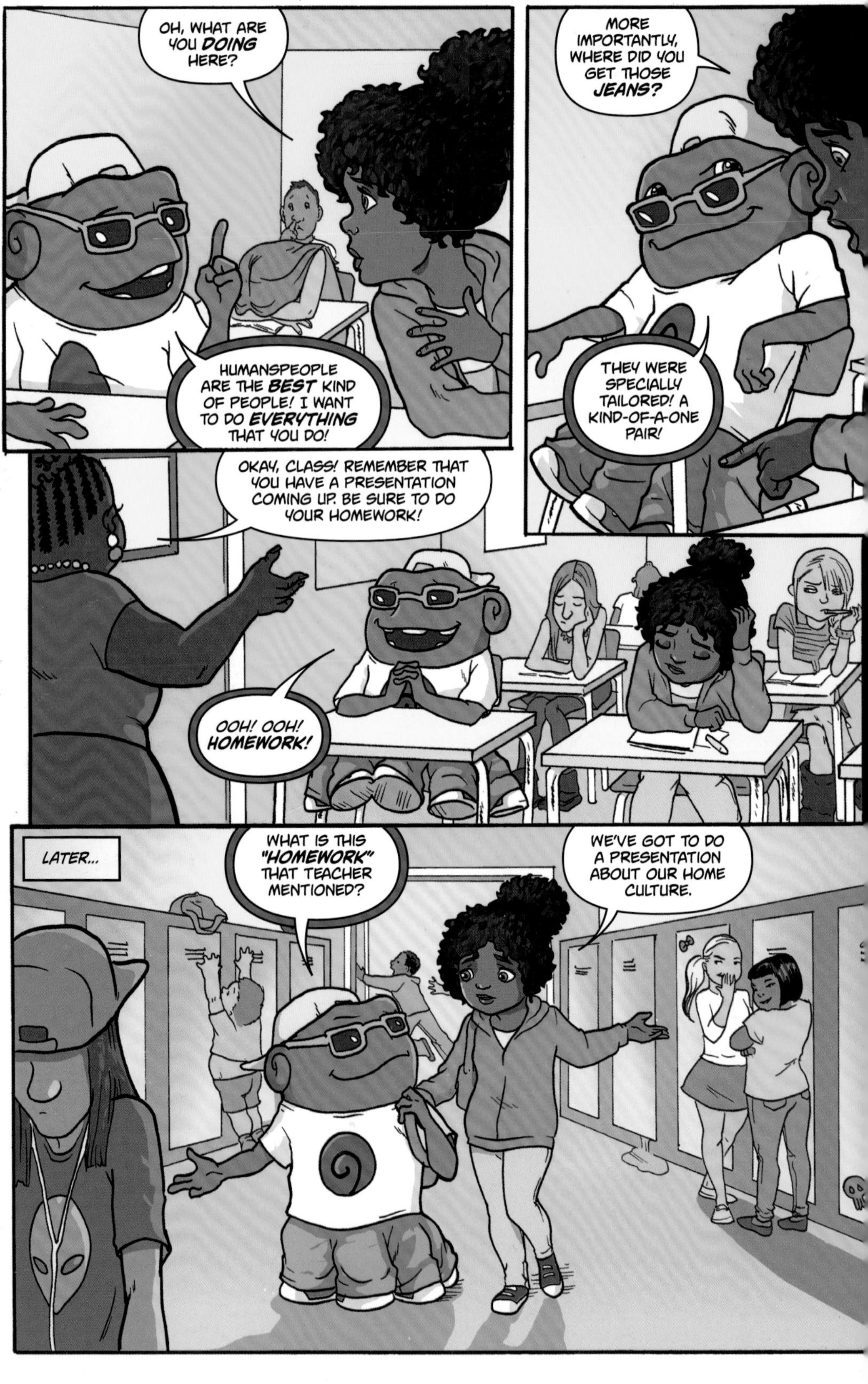
OH, WHAT ARE YOU DOING HERE?
HUMANSPEOPLE ARE THE BEST KIND OF PEOPLE! I WANT TO DO EVERYTHING THAT YOU DO!
MORE IMPORTANTLY, WHERE DID YOU GET THOSE JEANS?
THEY WERE SPECIALLY TAILORED! A KIND-OF-A-ONE PAIR!
OKAY, CLASS! REMEMBER THAT YOU HAVE A PRESENTATION COMING UP. BE SURE TO DO YOUR HOMEWORK!
OOH! OOH! HOMEWORK!
LATER...
WHAT IS THIS "HOMEWORK" THAT TEACHER MENTIONED?
WE'VE GOT TO DO A PRESENTATION ABOUT OUR HOME CULTURE.

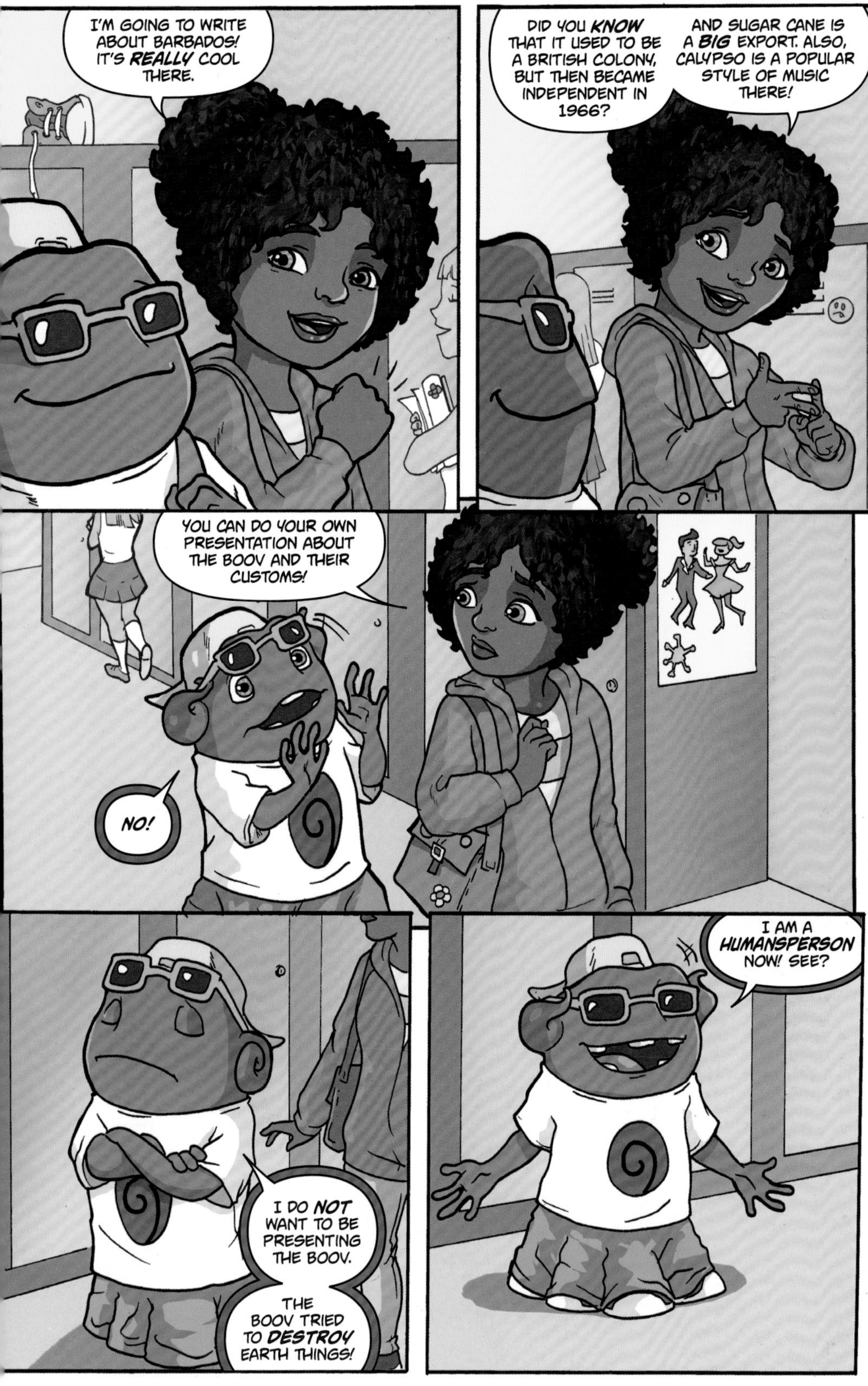
I'M GOING TO WRITE ABOUT BARBADOS! IT'S REALLY COOL THERE.
DID YOU KNOW THAT IT USED TO BE A BRITISH COLONY, BUT THEN BECAME INDEPENDENT IN 1966?
AND SUGAR CANE IS A BIG EXPORT. ALSO, CALYPSO IS A POPULAR STYLE OF MUSIC THERE!
YOU CAN DO YOUR OWN PRESENTATION ABOUT THE BOOV AND THEIR CUSTOMS!
NO!
I DO NOT WANT TO BE PRESENTING THE BOOV.
THE BOOV TRIED TO DESTROY EARTH THINGS!
I AM A HUMANSPERSON NOW! SEE?

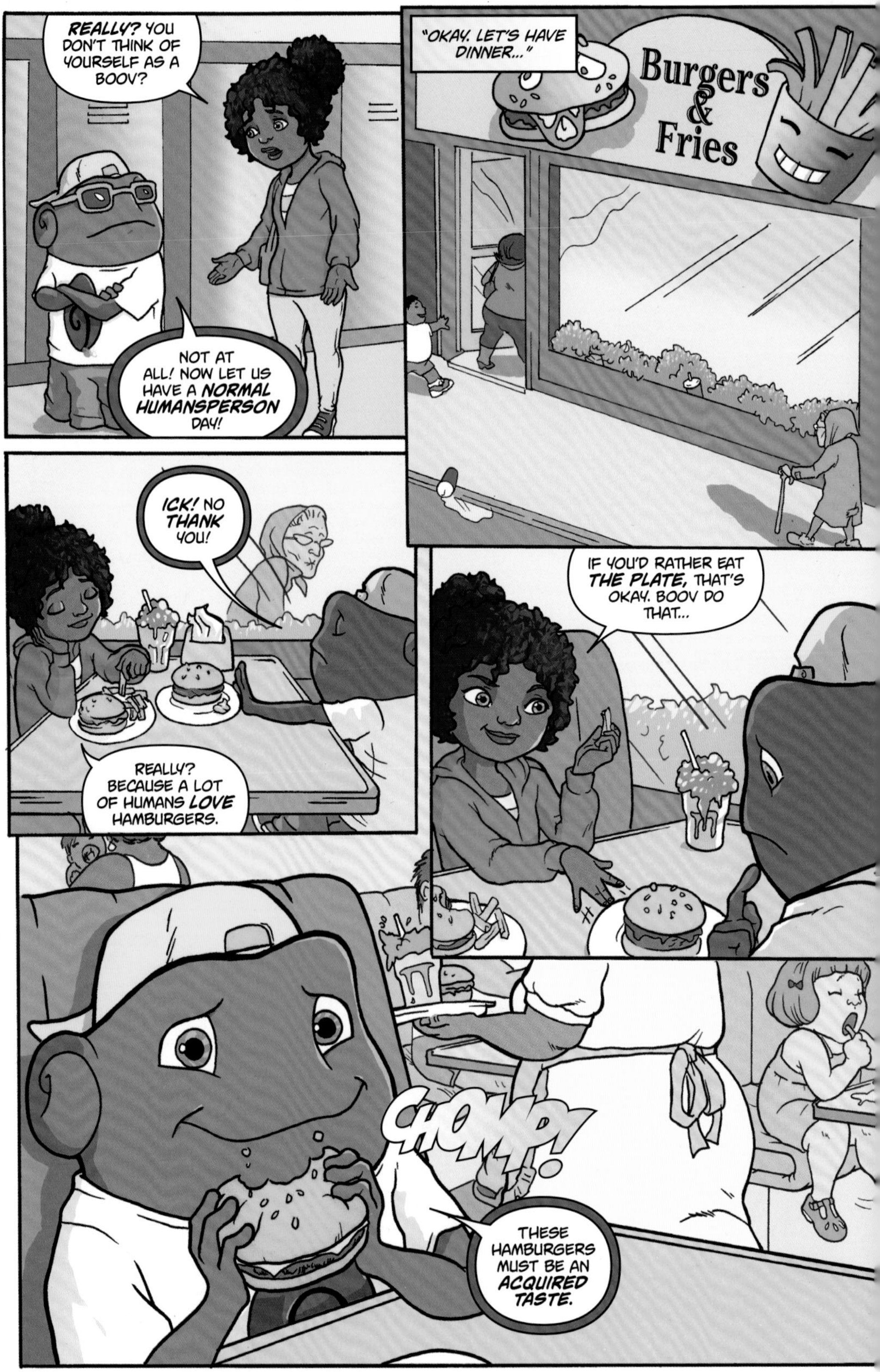
REALLY? YOU DON'T THINK OF YOURSELF AS A BOOV?
NOT AT ALL! NOW LET US HAVE A NORMAL HUMANSPERSON DAY!
"OKAY. LET'S HAVE DINNER..."
Burgers & Fries
ICK! NO THANK YOU!
REALLY? BECAUSE A LOT OF HUMANS LOVE HAMBURGERS.
IF YOU'D RATHER EAT THE PLATE, THAT'S OKAY. BOOV DO THAT...
CHOMP!
THESE HAMBURGERS MUST BE AN ACQUIRED TASTE.

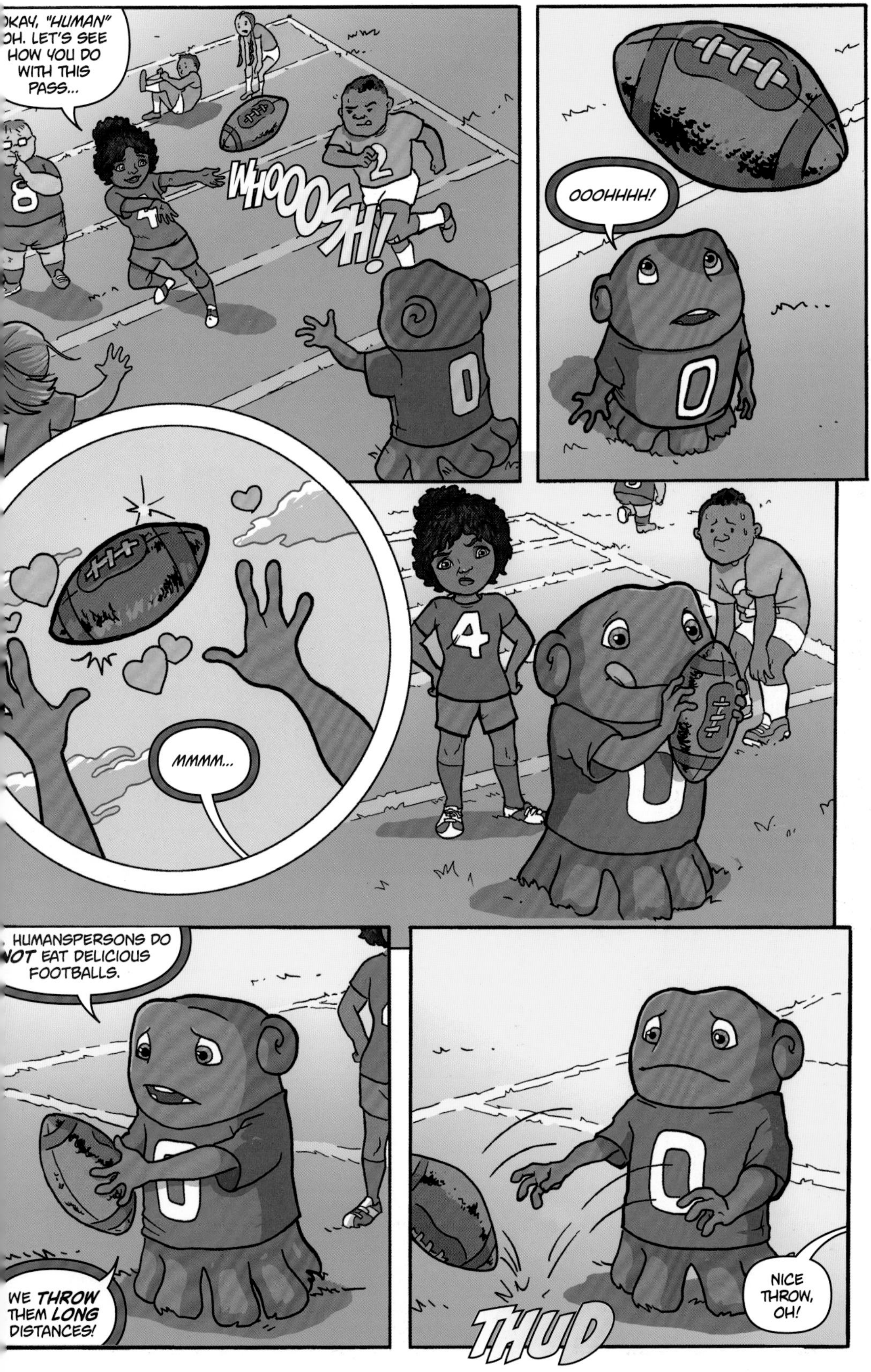
OKAY, "HUMAN" OH. LET'S SEE HOW YOU DO WITH THIS PASS...
WHOOOSH!
OOOHHHH!
MMMM...
HUMANSPERSONS DO NOT EAT DELICIOUS FOOTBALLS.
WE THROW THEM LONG DISTANCES!
THUD
NICE THROW, OH!

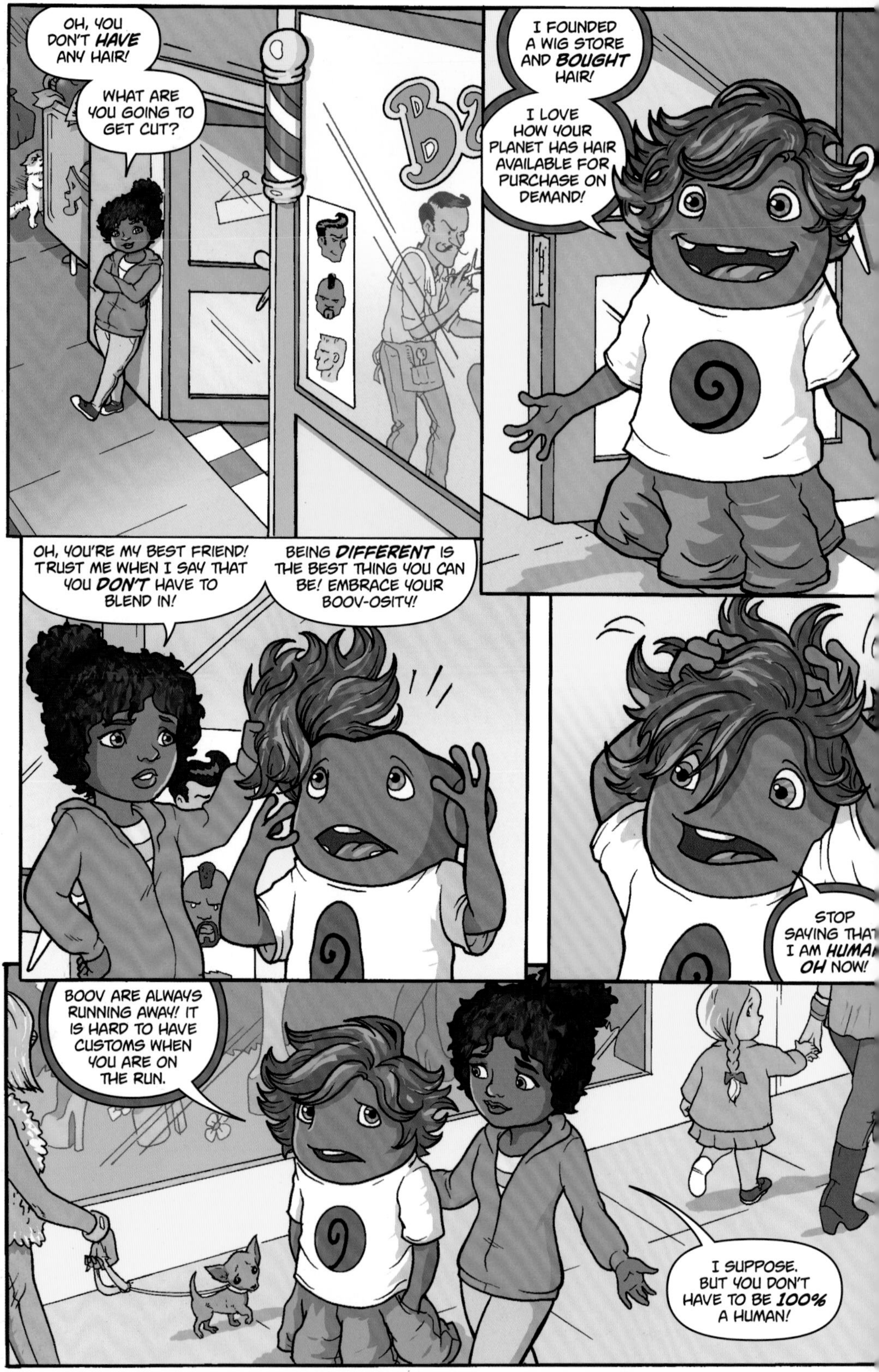
OH, YOU DON'T HAVE ANY HAIR!
WHAT ARE YOU GOING TO GET CUT?
I FOUNDED A WIG STORE AND BOUGHT HAIR!
I LOVE HOW YOUR PLANET HAS HAIR AVAILABLE FOR PURCHASE ON DEMAND!
OH, YOU'RE MY BEST FRIEND! TRUST ME WHEN I SAY THAT YOU DON'T HAVE TO BLEND IN!
BEING DIFFERENT IS THE BEST THING YOU CAN BE! EMBRACE YOUR BOOV-OSITY!
STOP SAYING THAT I AM HUMAN OH NOW!
BOOV ARE ALWAYS RUNNING AWAY! IT IS HARD TO HAVE CUSTOMS WHEN YOU ARE ON THE RUN.
I SUPPOSE. BUT YOU DON'T HAVE TO BE 100% A HUMAN!

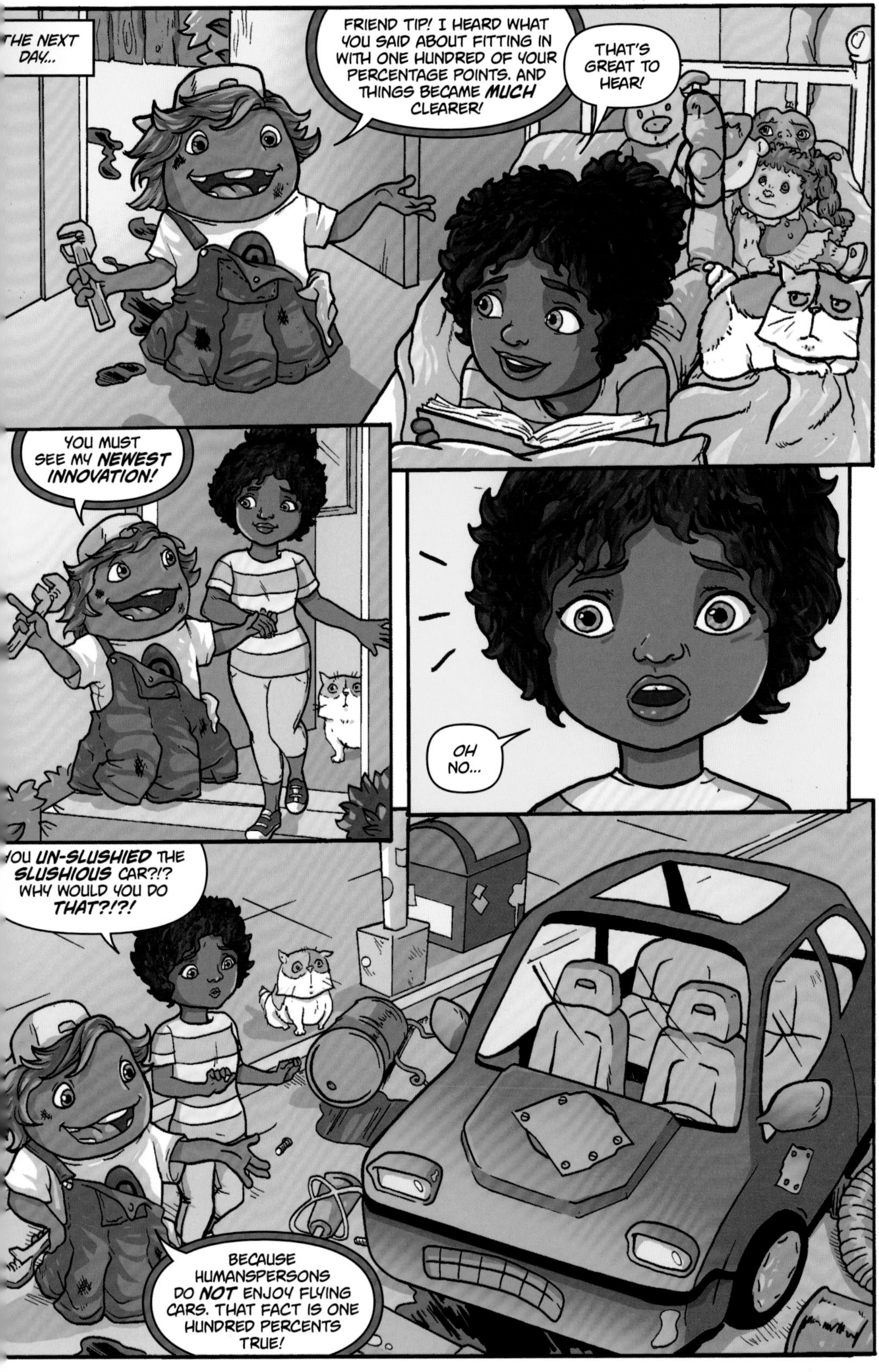
THE NEXT DAY...
FRIEND TIP! I HEARD WHAT YOU SAID ABOUT FITTING IN WITH ONE HUNDRED OF YOUR PERCENTAGE POINTS. AND THINGS BECAME MUCH CLEARER!
THAT'S GREAT TO HEAR!
YOU MUST SEE MY NEWEST INNOVATION!
OH NO...
YOU UN-SLUSHIED THE SLUSHIOUS CAR?!? WHY WOULD YOU DO THAT?!?!
BECAUSE HUMANSPERSONS DO NOT ENJOY FLYING CARS. THAT FACT IS ONE HUNDRED PERCENTS TRUE!

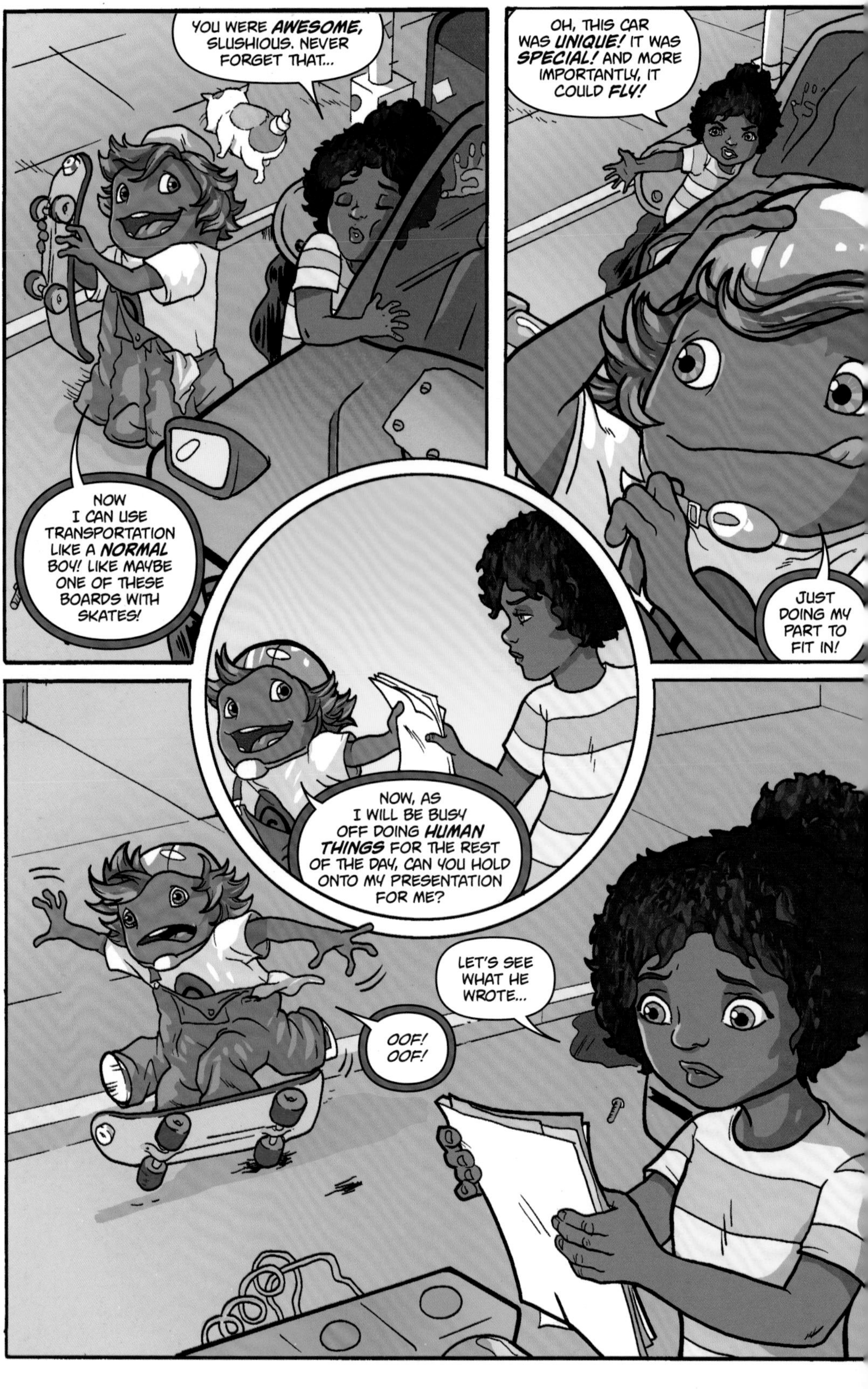
YOU WERE AWESOME, SLUSHIOUS. NEVER FORGET THAT...
NOW I CAN USE TRANSPORTATION LIKE A NORMAL BOY! LIKE MAYBE ONE OF THESE BOARDS WITH SKATES!
OH, THIS CAR WAS UNIQUE! IT WAS SPECIAL! AND MORE IMPORTANTLY, IT COULD FLY!
JUST DOING MY PART TO FIT IN!
NOW, AS I WILL BE BUSY OFF DOING HUMAN THINGS FOR THE REST OF THE DAY, CAN YOU HOLD ONTO MY PRESENTATION FOR ME?
LET'S SEE WHAT HE WROTE...
OOF! OOF!

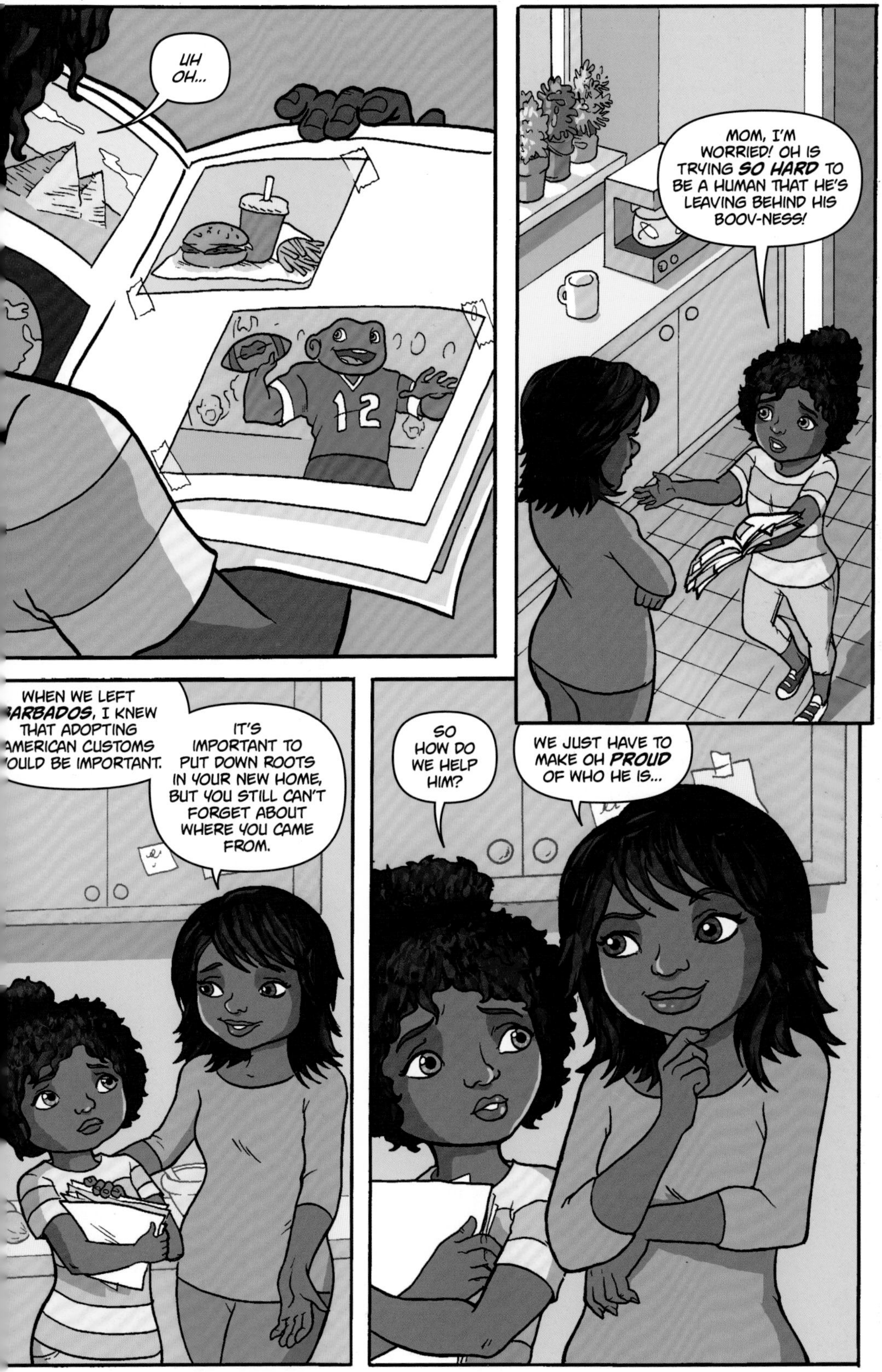
UH OH...
12
MOM, I'M WORRIED! OH IS TRYING **SO HARD** TO BE A HUMAN THAT HE'S LEAVING BEHIND HIS BOOV-NESS!
WHEN WE LEFT *BARBADOS*, I KNEW THAT ADOPTING AMERICAN CUSTOMS WOULD BE IMPORTANT.
IT'S IMPORTANT TO PUT DOWN ROOTS IN YOUR NEW HOME, BUT YOU STILL CAN'T FORGET ABOUT WHERE YOU CAME FROM.
SO HOW DO WE HELP HIM?
WE JUST HAVE TO MAKE OH **PROUD** OF WHO HE IS...

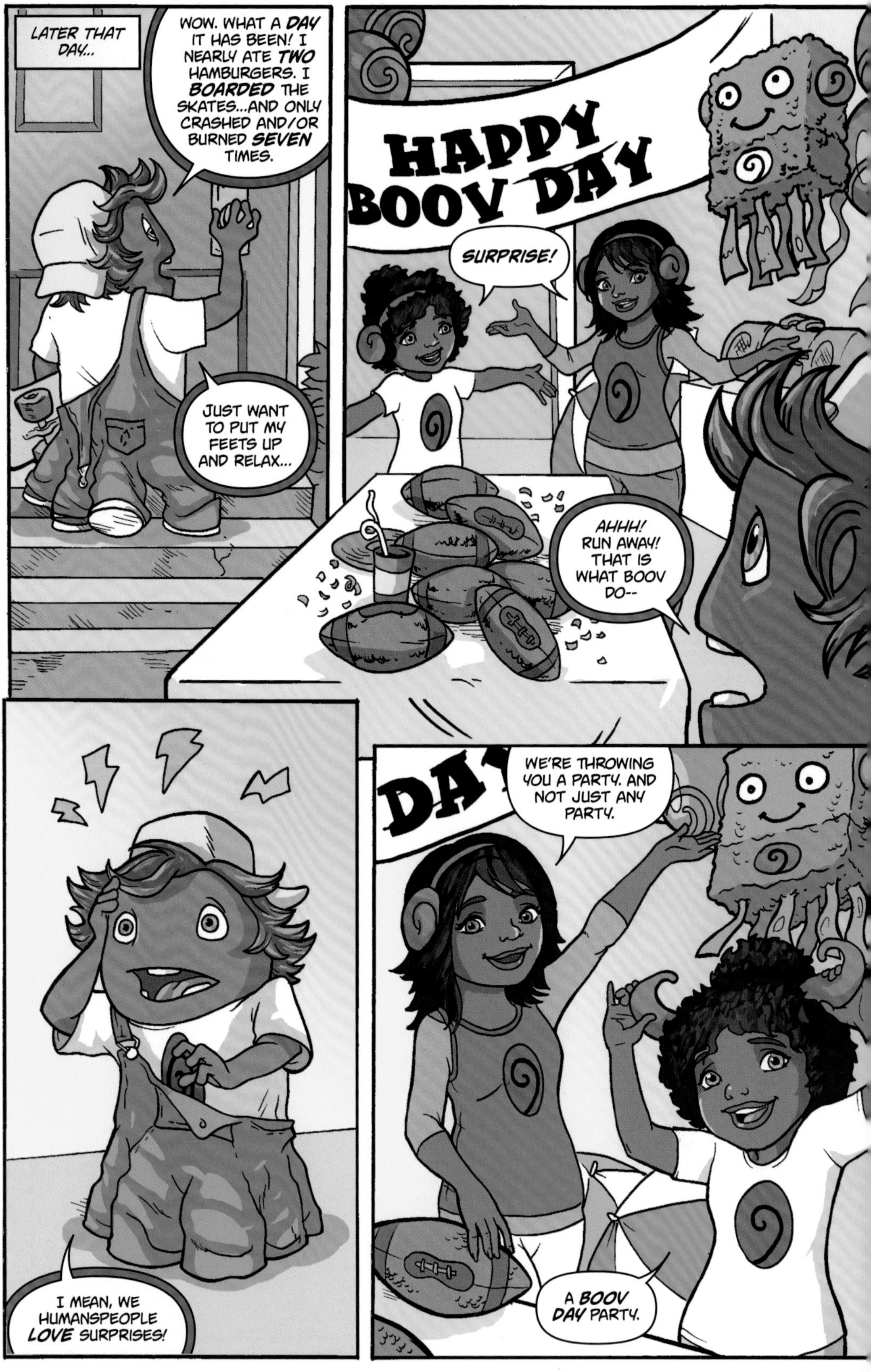
LATER THAT DAY...
WOW. WHAT A DAY IT HAS BEEN! I NEARLY ATE TWO HAMBURGERS. I BOARDED THE SKATES...AND ONLY CRASHED AND/OR BURNED SEVEN TIMES.
JUST WANT TO PUT MY FEETS UP AND RELAX...
HAPPY BOOV DAY
SURPRISE!
AHHH! RUN AWAY! THAT IS WHAT BOOV DO--
I MEAN, WE HUMANSPEOPLE LOVE SURPRISES!
WE'RE THROWING YOU A PARTY. AND NOT JUST ANY PARTY.
A BOOV DAY PARTY.

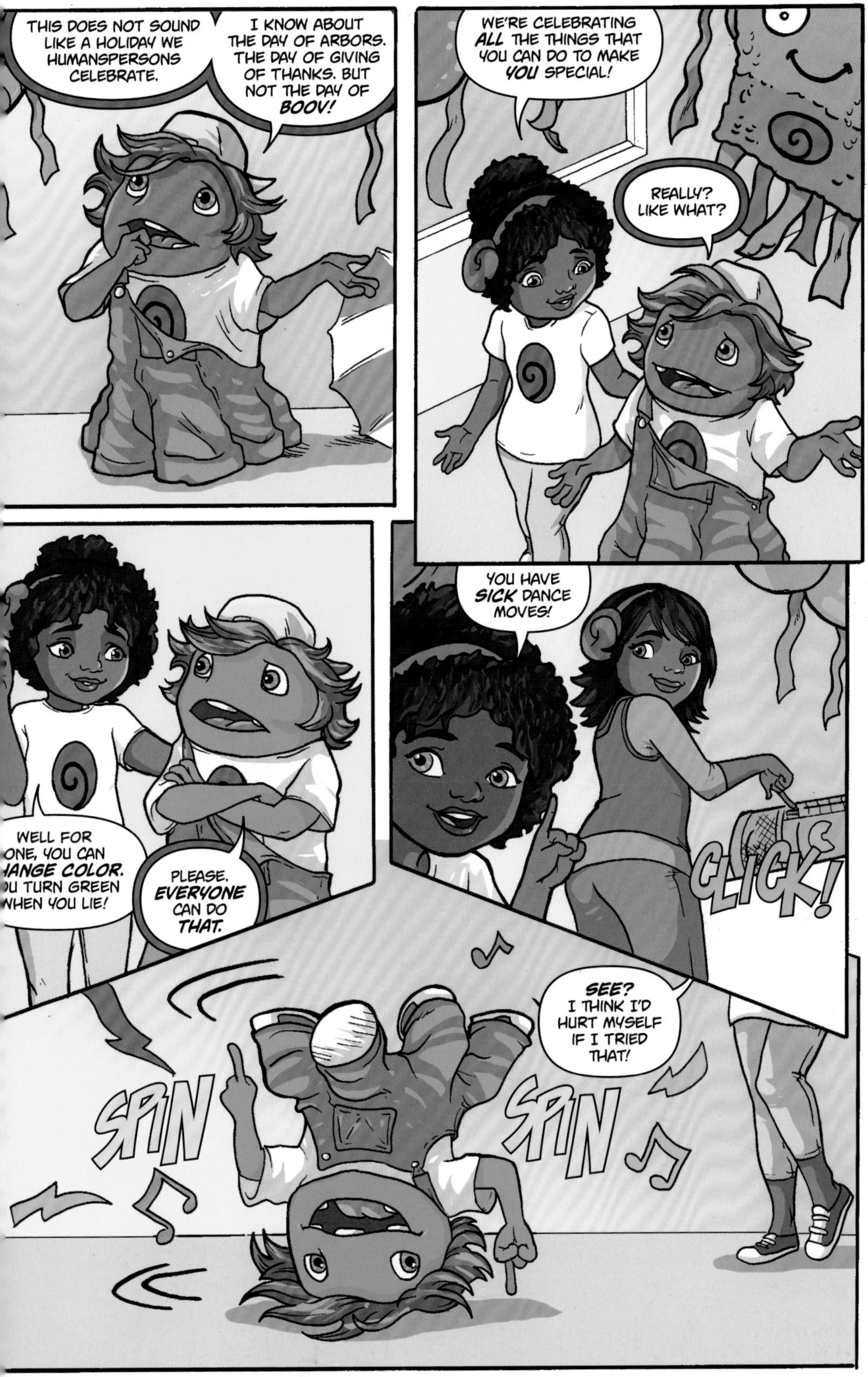
THIS DOES NOT SOUND LIKE A HOLIDAY WE HUMANSPERSONS CELEBRATE.
I KNOW ABOUT THE DAY OF ARBORS. THE DAY OF GIVING OF THANKS. BUT NOT THE DAY OF BOOV!
WE'RE CELEBRATING ALL THE THINGS THAT YOU CAN DO TO MAKE YOU SPECIAL!
REALLY? LIKE WHAT?
WELL FOR ONE, YOU CAN HANGE COLOR. OU TURN GREEN WHEN YOU LIE!
PLEASE. EVERYONE CAN DO THAT.
YOU HAVE SICK DANCE MOVES!
CLICK!
SPIN
SPIN
SEE? I THINK I'D HURT MYSELF IF I TRIED THAT!

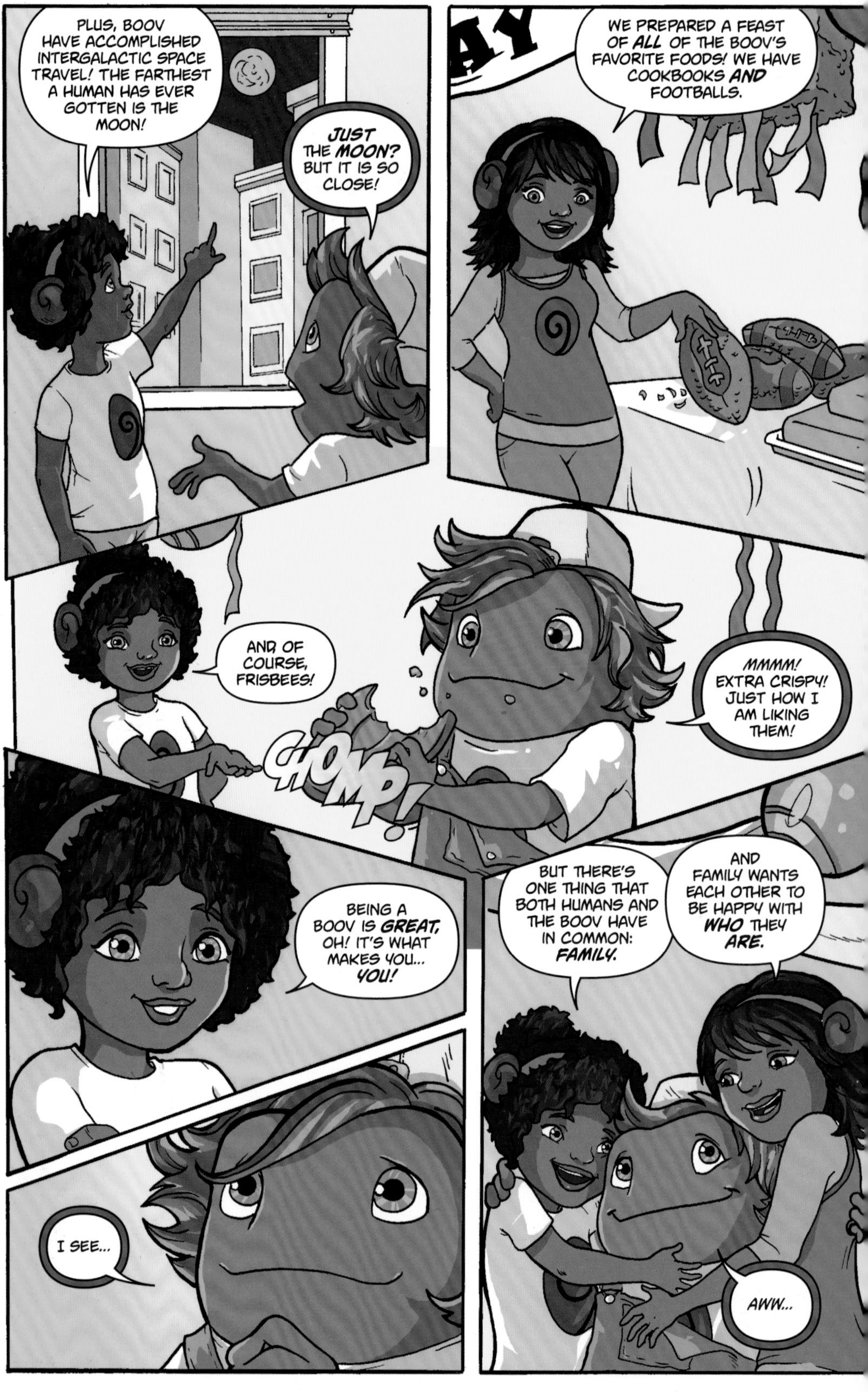
PLUS, BOOV HAVE ACCOMPLISHED INTERGALACTIC SPACE TRAVEL! THE FARTHEST A HUMAN HAS EVER GOTTEN IS THE MOON!
JUST THE MOON? BUT IT IS SO CLOSE!
WE PREPARED A FEAST OF ALL OF THE BOOV'S FAVORITE FOODS! WE HAVE COOKBOOKS AND FOOTBALLS.
AND OF COURSE, FRISBEES!
CHOMP!
MMMM! EXTRA CRISPY! JUST HOW I AM LIKING THEM!
BEING A BOOV IS GREAT, OH! IT'S WHAT MAKES YOU... YOU!
I SEE...
BUT THERE'S ONE THING THAT BOTH HUMANS AND THE BOOV HAVE IN COMMON: FAMILY.
AND FAMILY WANTS EACH OTHER TO BE HAPPY WITH WHO THEY ARE.
AWW...

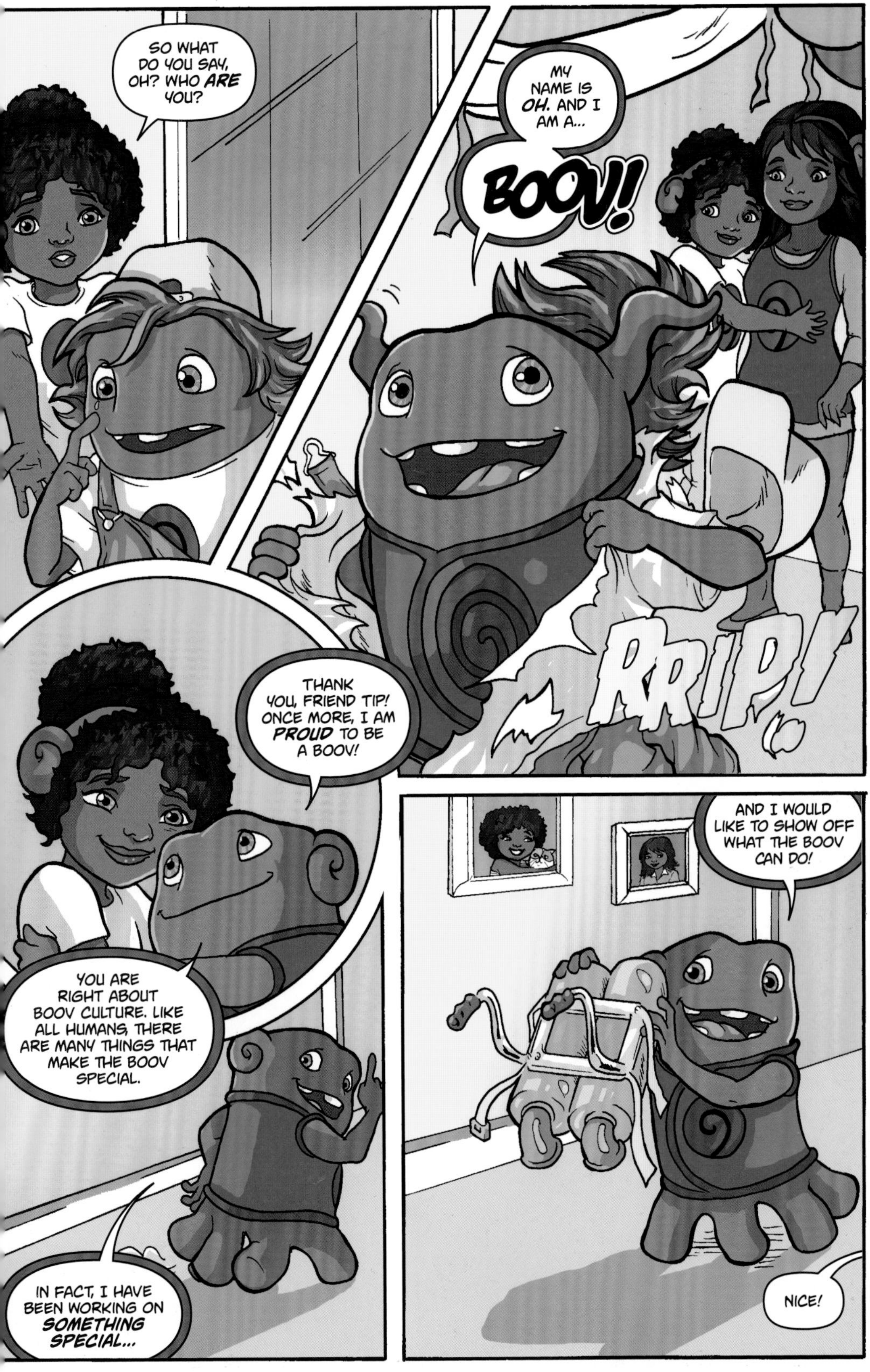
SO WHAT DO YOU SAY, OH? WHO ARE YOU?
MY NAME IS OH. AND I AM A...
BOOV!
RRIP!
THANK YOU, FRIEND TIP! ONCE MORE, I AM PROUD TO BE A BOOV!
YOU ARE RIGHT ABOUT BOOV CULTURE. LIKE ALL HUMANS, THERE ARE MANY THINGS THAT MAKE THE BOOV SPECIAL.
IN FACT, I HAVE BEEN WORKING ON SOMETHING SPECIAL...
AND I WOULD LIKE TO SHOW OFF WHAT THE BOOV CAN DO!
NICE!

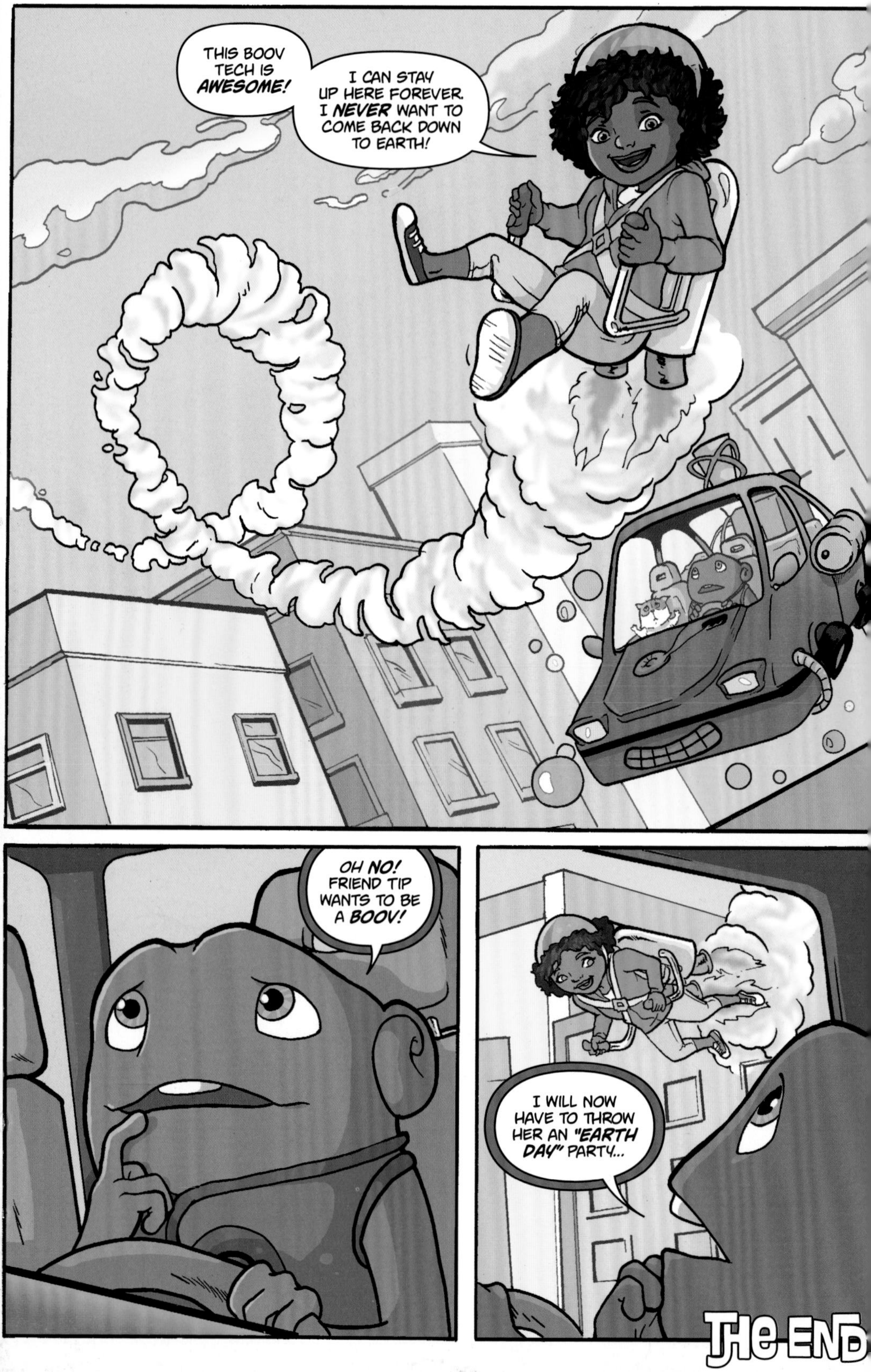
THIS BOOV TECH IS AWESOME!
I CAN STAY UP HERE FOREVER. I NEVER WANT TO COME BACK DOWN TO EARTH!
OH NO! FRIEND TIP WANTS TO BE A BOOV!
I WILL NOW HAVE TO THROW HER AN "EARTH DAY" PARTY...
THE END

ANOTHER HOME

WRITER
Max Davison
ART
Nigel Auchterlounie
LETTERS
Jim Campbell

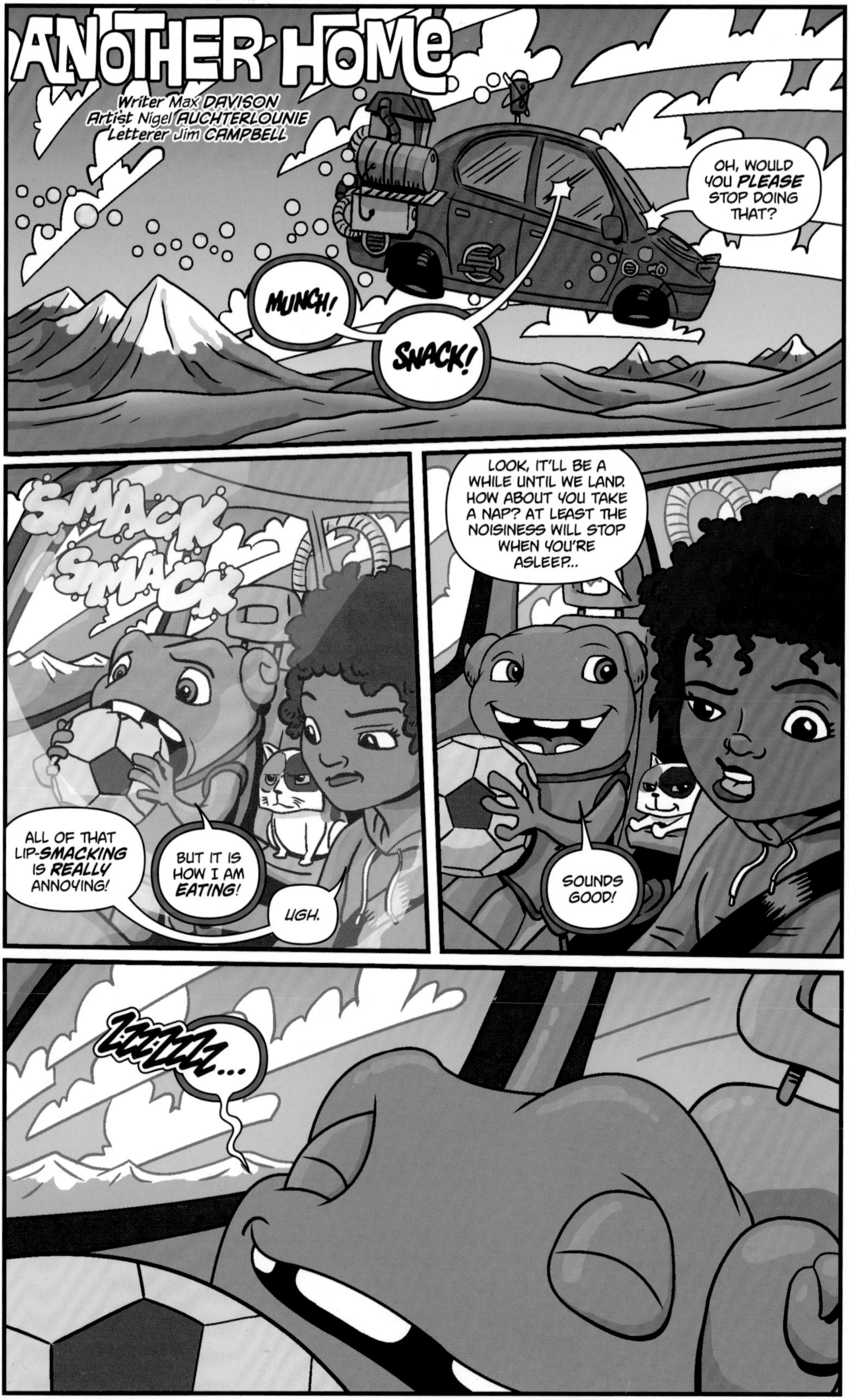
ANOTHER HOME
Writer Max DAVISON
Artist Nigel AUCHTERLOUNIE
Letterer Jim CAMPBELL
MUNCH!
SNACK!
OH, WOULD YOU PLEASE STOP DOING THAT?
SMACK SMACK
ALL OF THAT LIP-SMACKING IS REALLY ANNOYING!
BUT IT IS HOW I AM EATING!
UGH.
LOOK, IT'LL BE A WHILE UNTIL WE LAND. HOW ABOUT YOU TAKE A NAP? AT LEAST THE NOISINESS WILL STOP WHEN YOU'RE ASLEEP...
SOUNDS GOOD!
ZZZZZZ...

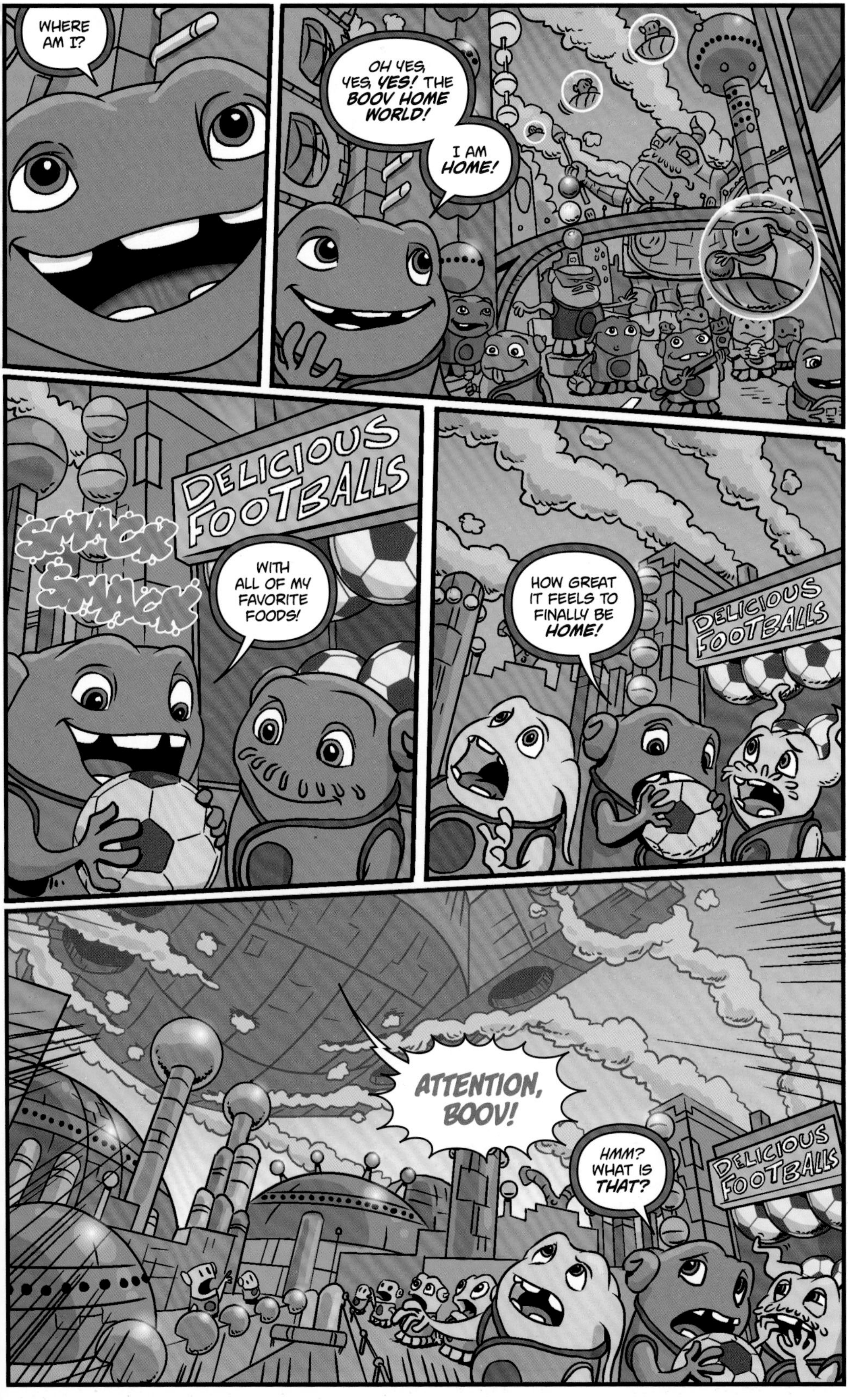
WHERE AM I?
OH YES, YES, YES! THE BOOV HOME WORLD!
I AM HOME!
DELICIOUS FOOTBALLS
SMACK SMACK
WITH ALL OF MY FAVORITE FOODS!
HOW GREAT IT FEELS TO FINALLY BE HOME!
DELICIOUS FOOTBALLS
ATTENTION, BOOV!
HMM? WHAT IS THAT?
DELICIOUS FOOTBALLS

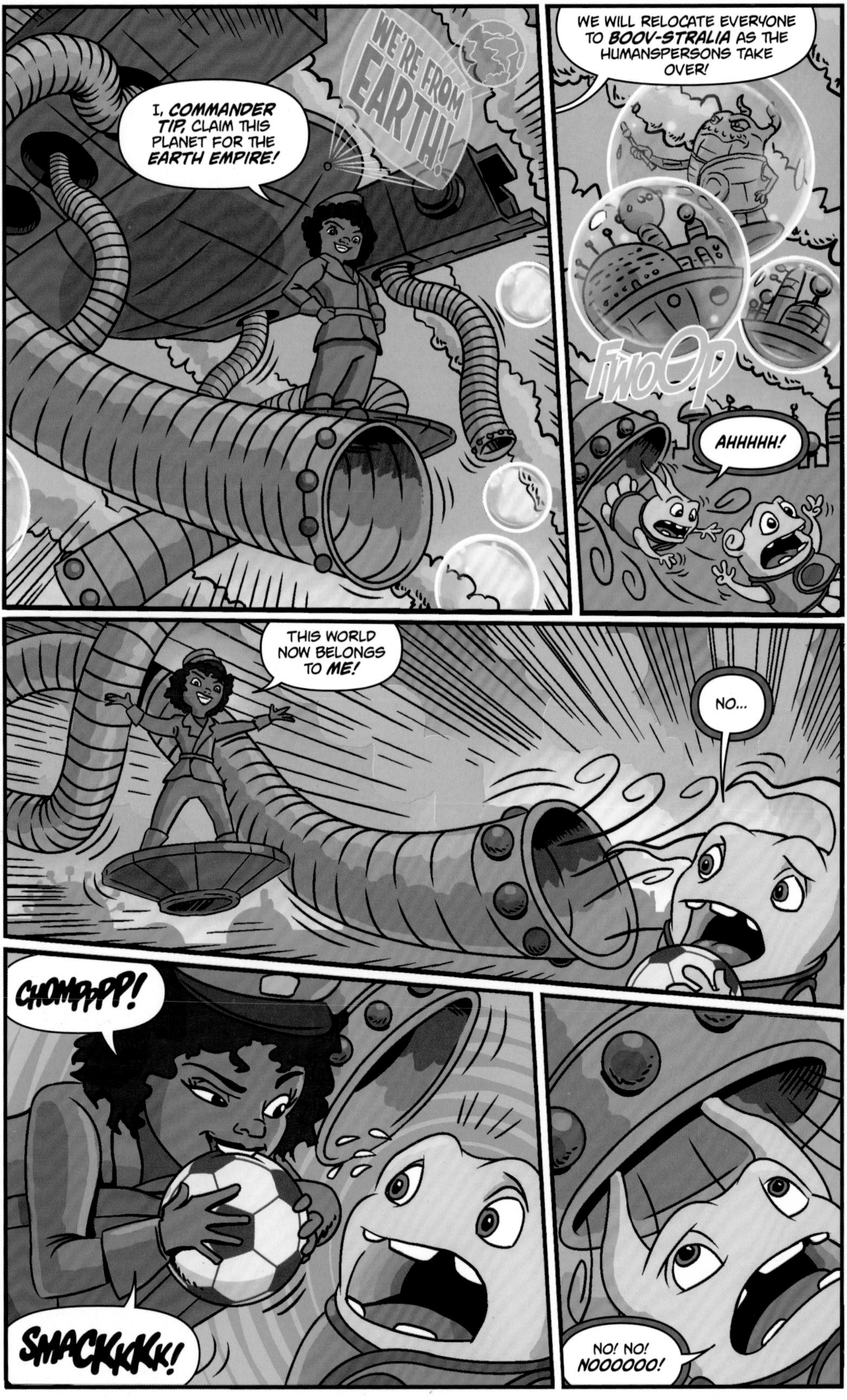
WE'RE FROM EARTH!
I, COMMANDER TIP, CLAIM THIS PLANET FOR THE EARTH EMPIRE!
WE WILL RELOCATE EVERYONE TO BOOV-STRALIA AS THE HUMANSPERSONS TAKE OVER!
FWOOP
AHHHHH!
THIS WORLD NOW BELONGS TO ME!
NO...
CHOMPPP!
SMACKKKK!
NO! NO! NOOOOOO!

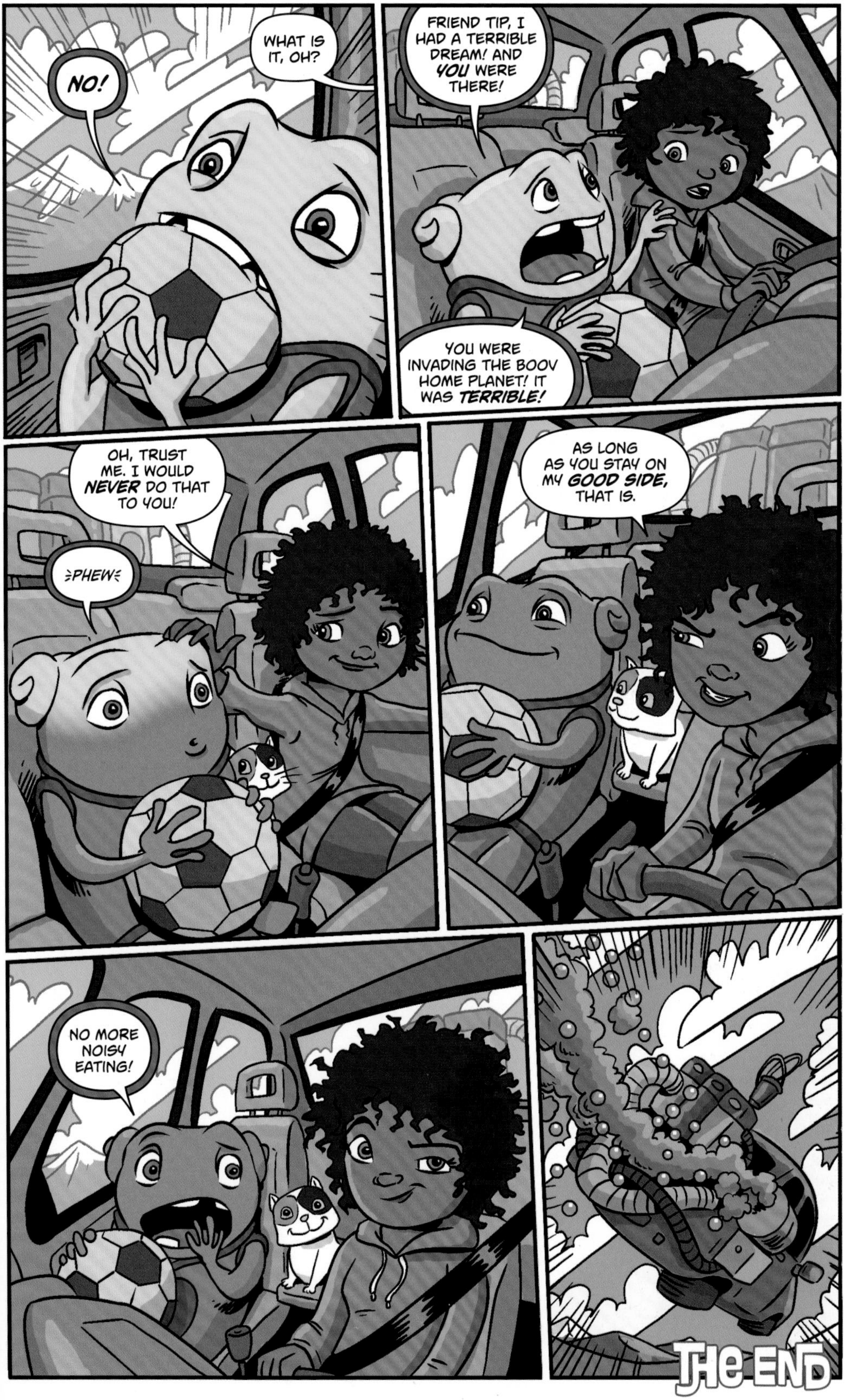
NO!
WHAT IS IT, OH?
FRIEND TIP, I HAD A TERRIBLE DREAM! AND YOU WERE THERE!
YOU WERE INVADING THE BOOV HOME PLANET! IT WAS TERRIBLE!
OH, TRUST ME. I WOULD NEVER DO THAT TO YOU!
PHEW
AS LONG AS YOU STAY ON MY GOOD SIDE, THAT IS.
NO MORE NOISY EATING!
THE END

Captain Smer
HAPPY
HUMANSTOW

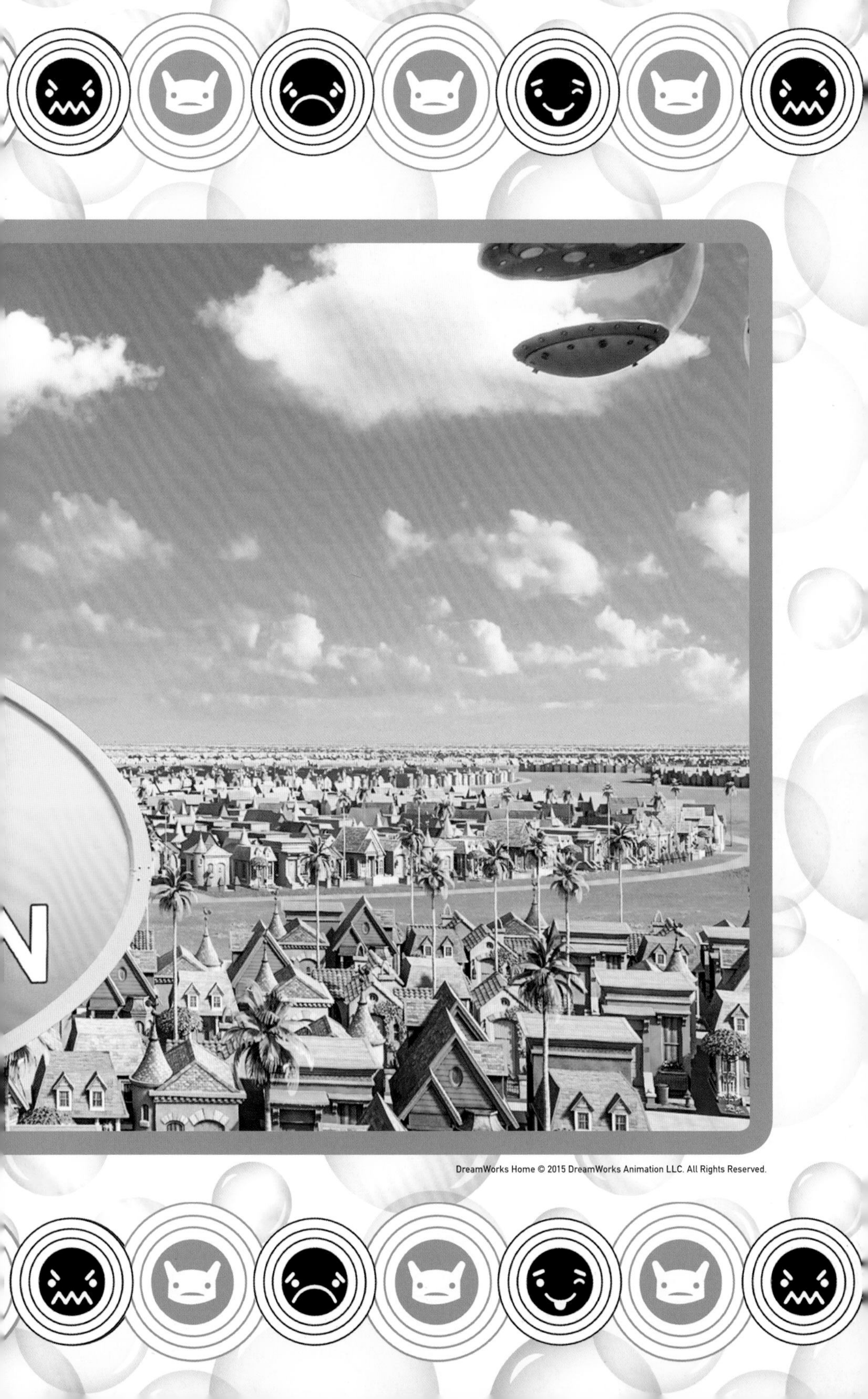

GHOST STORIES

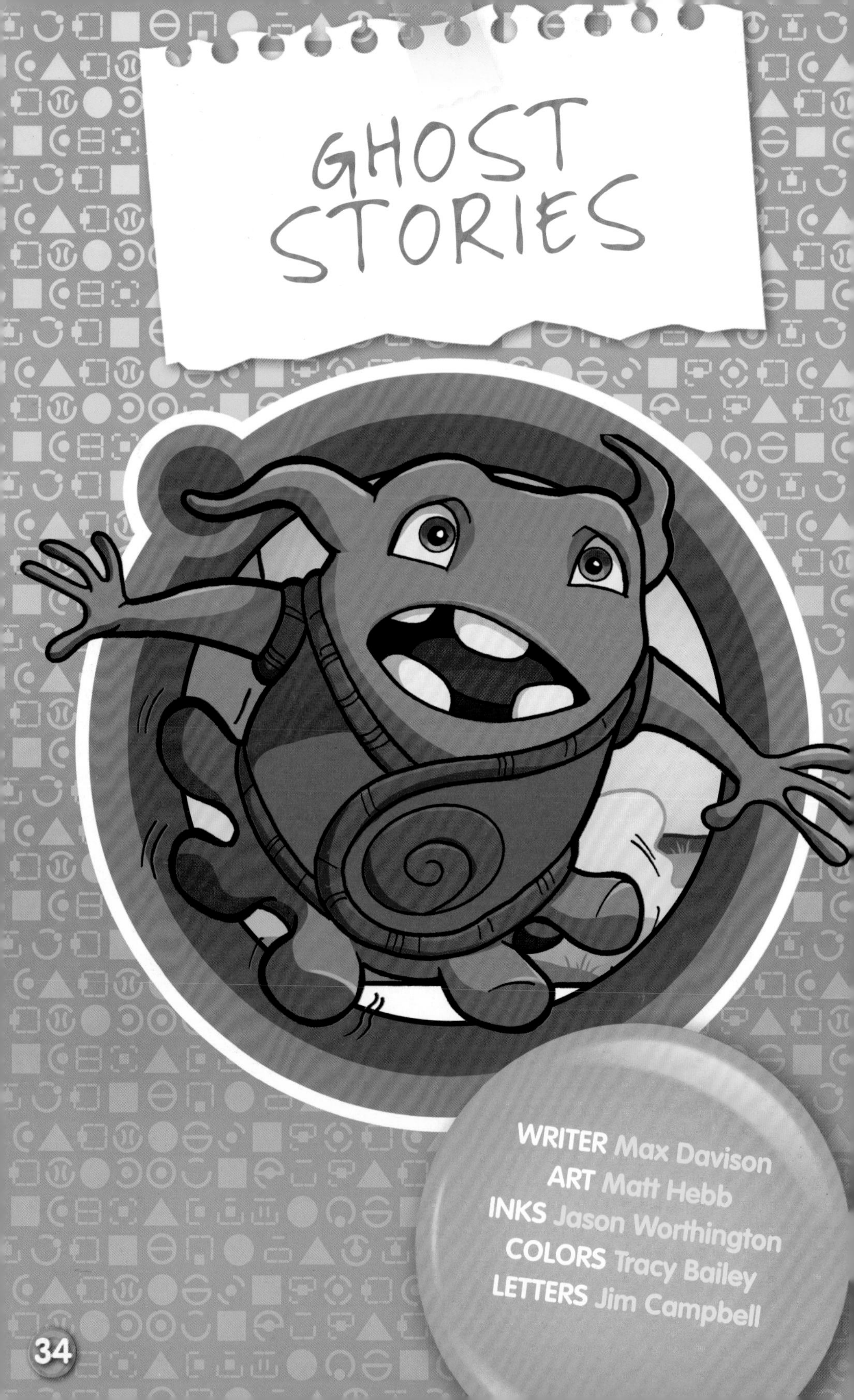

WRITER Max Davison
ART Matt Hebb
INKS Jason Worthington
COLORS Tracy Bailey
LETTERS Jim Campbell

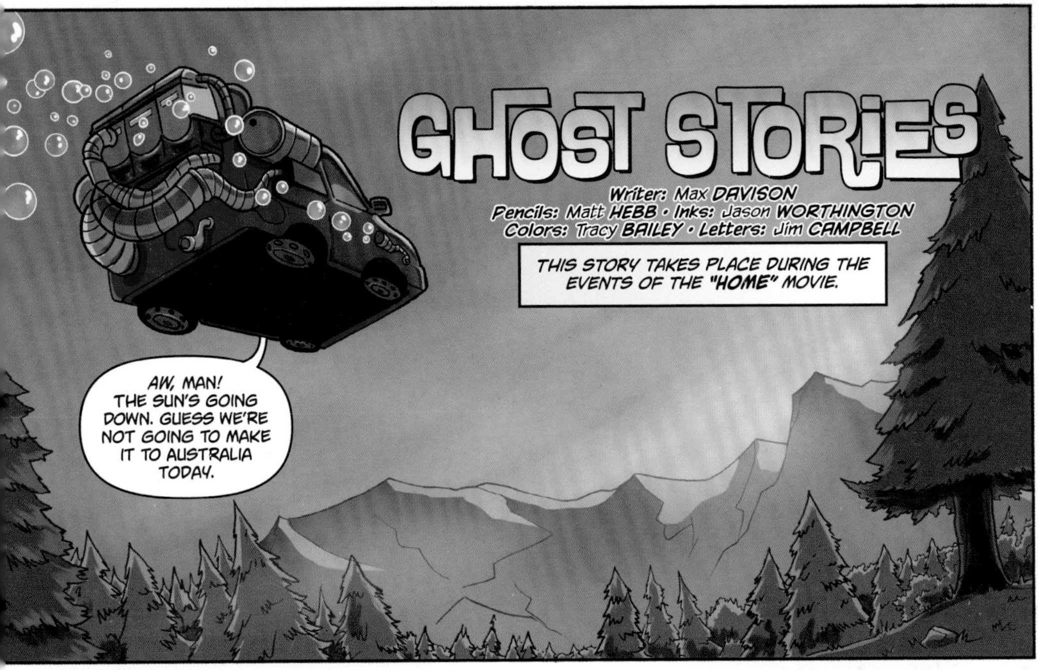
GHOST STORIES
Writer: Max DAVISON
Pencils: Matt HEBB • Inks: Jason WORTHINGTON
Colors: Tracy BAILEY • Letters: Jim CAMPBELL
THIS STORY TAKES PLACE DURING THE EVENTS OF THE "HOME" MOVIE.
AW, MAN! THE SUN'S GOING DOWN. GUESS WE'RE NOT GOING TO MAKE IT TO AUSTRALIA TODAY.

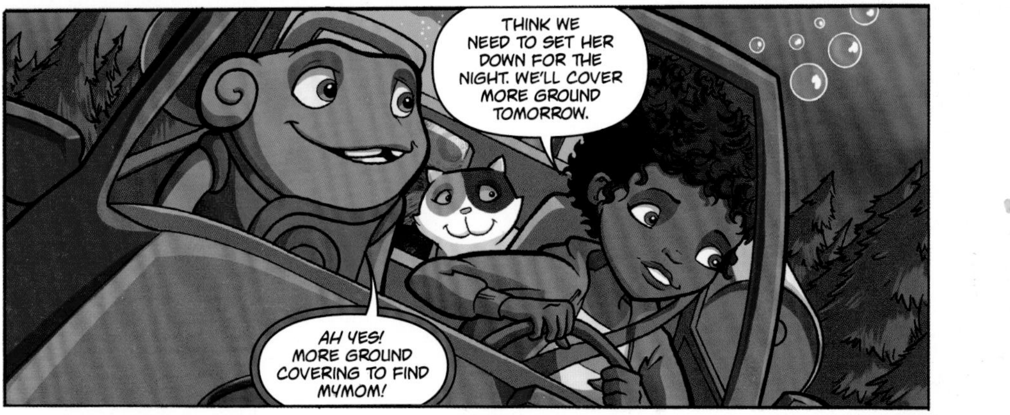
THINK WE NEED TO SET HER DOWN FOR THE NIGHT. WE'LL COVER MORE GROUND TOMORROW.
AH YES! MORE GROUND COVERING TO FIND MYMOM!

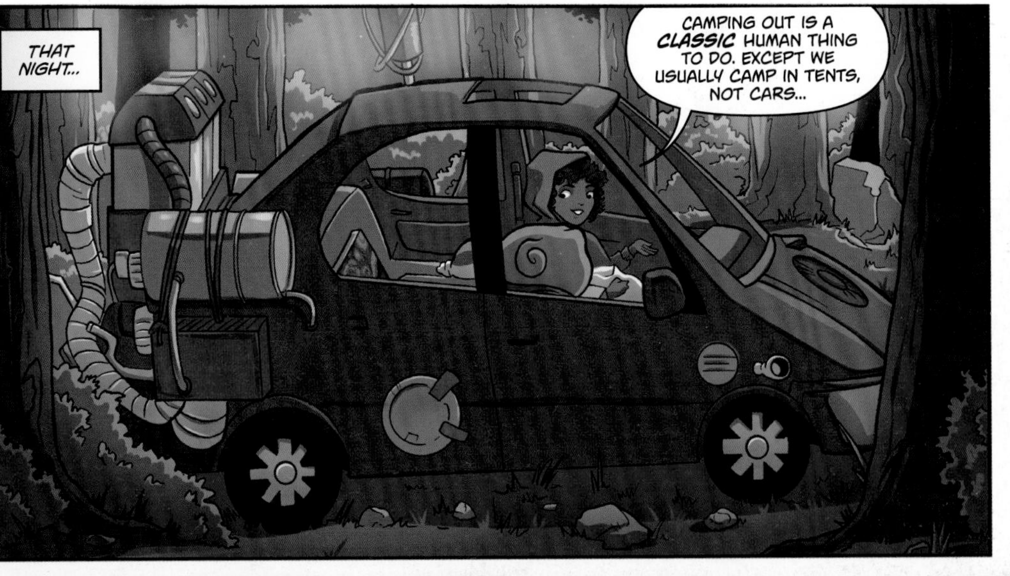
THAT NIGHT...
CAMPING OUT IS A CLASSIC HUMAN THING TO DO. EXCEPT WE USUALLY CAMP IN TENTS, NOT CARS...

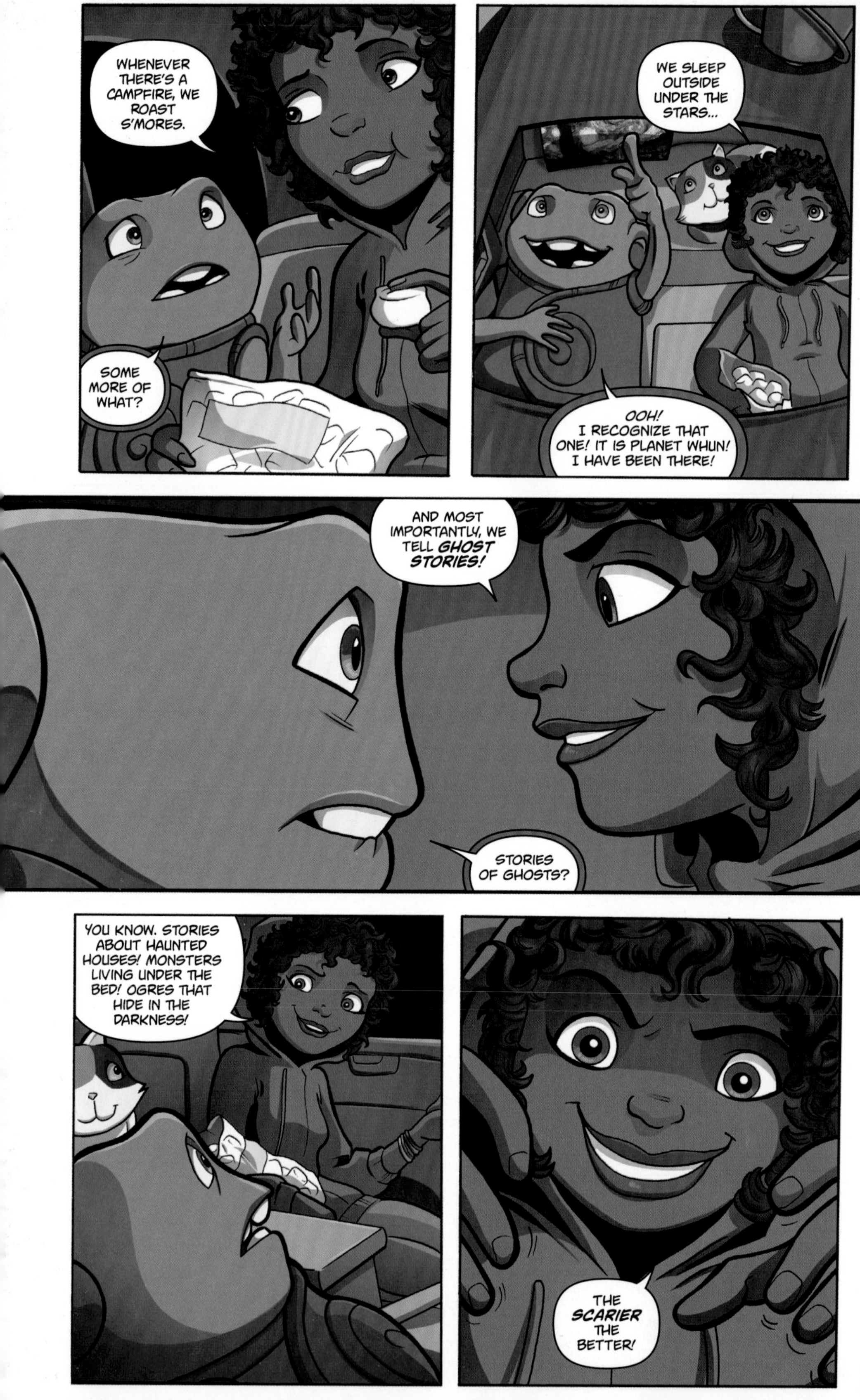
WHENEVER THERE'S A CAMPFIRE, WE ROAST S'MORES.
SOME MORE OF WHAT?
WE SLEEP OUTSIDE UNDER THE STARS...
OOH! I RECOGNIZE THAT ONE! IT IS PLANET WHUN! I HAVE BEEN THERE!
AND MOST IMPORTANTLY, WE TELL GHOST STORIES!
STORIES OF GHOSTS?
YOU KNOW. STORIES ABOUT HAUNTED HOUSES! MONSTERS LIVING UNDER THE BED! OGRES THAT HIDE IN THE DARKNESS!
THE SCARIER THE BETTER!

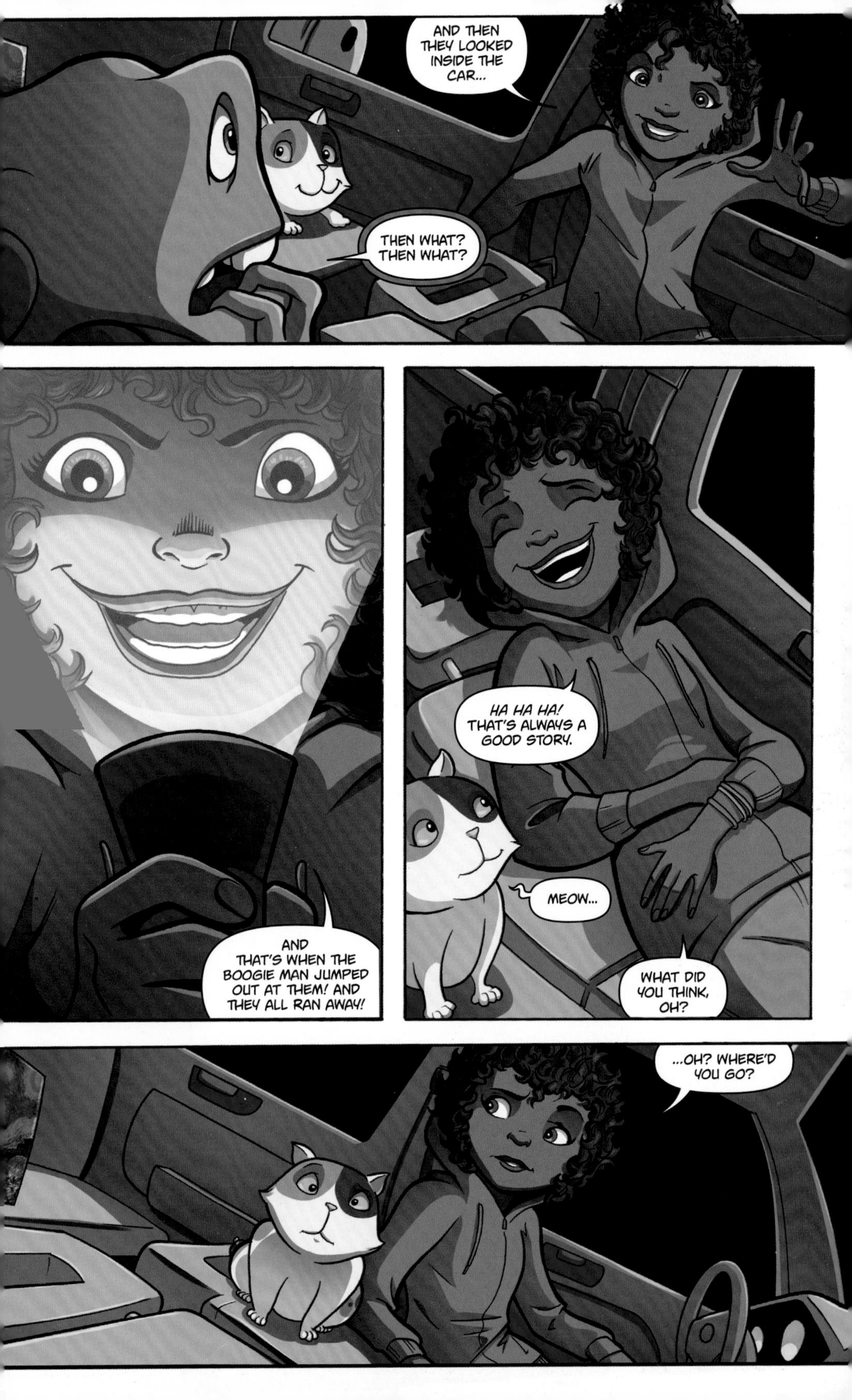
AND THEN THEY LOOKED INSIDE THE CAR...
THEN WHAT? THEN WHAT?
AND THAT'S WHEN THE BOOGIE MAN JUMPED OUT AT THEM! AND THEY ALL RAN AWAY!
HA HA HA! THAT'S ALWAYS A GOOD STORY.
MEOW...
WHAT DID YOU THINK, OH?
...OH? WHERE'D YOU GO?

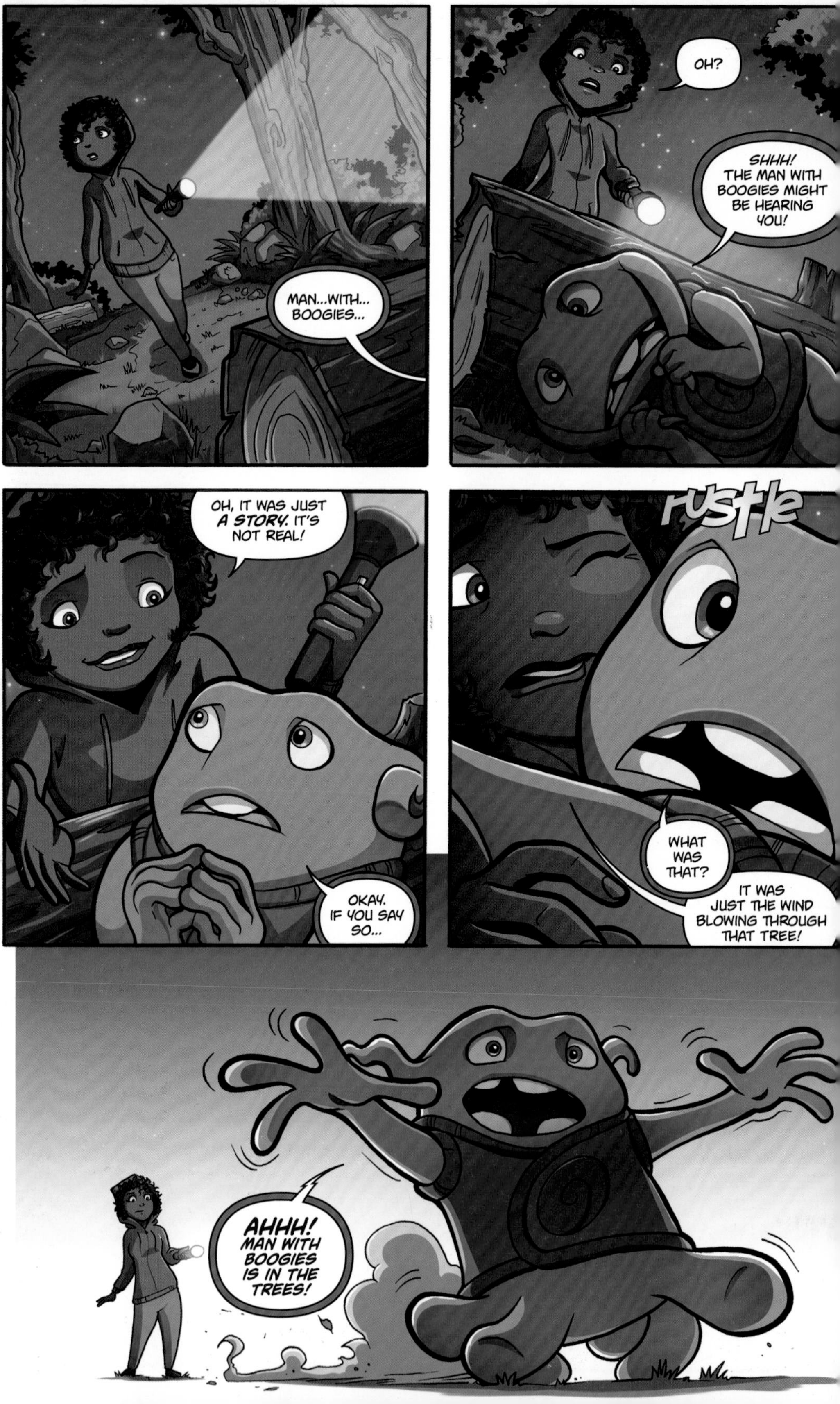
MAN...WITH... BOOGIES...
OH?
SHHH! THE MAN WITH BOOGIES MIGHT BE HEARING YOU!
OH, IT WAS JUST A *STORY*. IT'S NOT REAL!
OKAY. IF YOU SAY SO...
rustle
WHAT WAS THAT?
IT WAS JUST THE WIND BLOWING THROUGH THAT TREE!
AHHH! MAN WITH BOOGIES IS IN THE TREES!

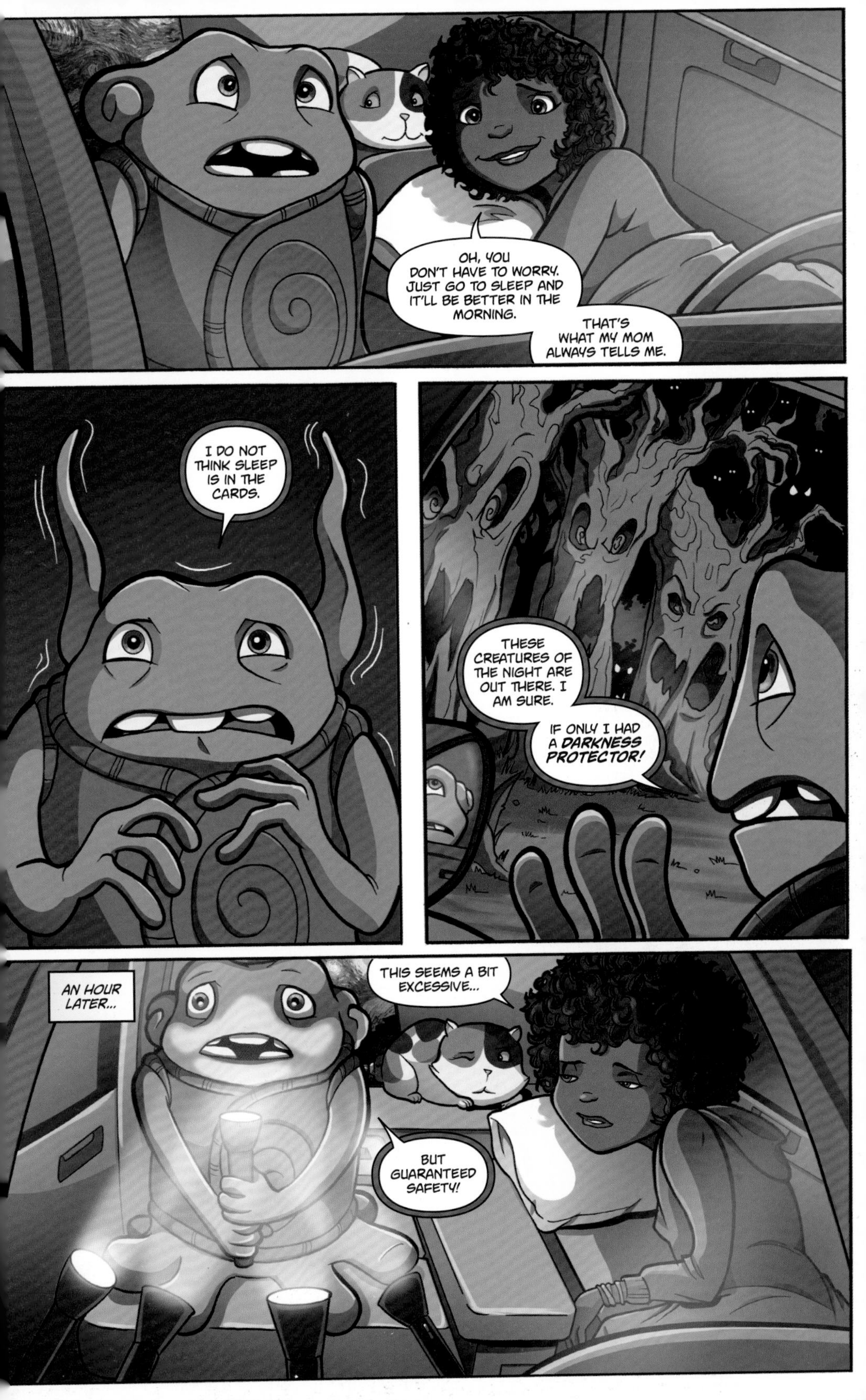
OH, YOU DON'T HAVE TO WORRY. JUST GO TO SLEEP AND IT'LL BE BETTER IN THE MORNING.
THAT'S WHAT MY MOM ALWAYS TELLS ME.
I DO NOT THINK SLEEP IS IN THE CARDS.
THESE CREATURES OF THE NIGHT ARE OUT THERE. I AM SURE.
IF ONLY I HAD A DARKNESS PROTECTOR!
AN HOUR LATER...
THIS SEEMS A BIT EXCESSIVE...
BUT GUARANTEED SAFETY!

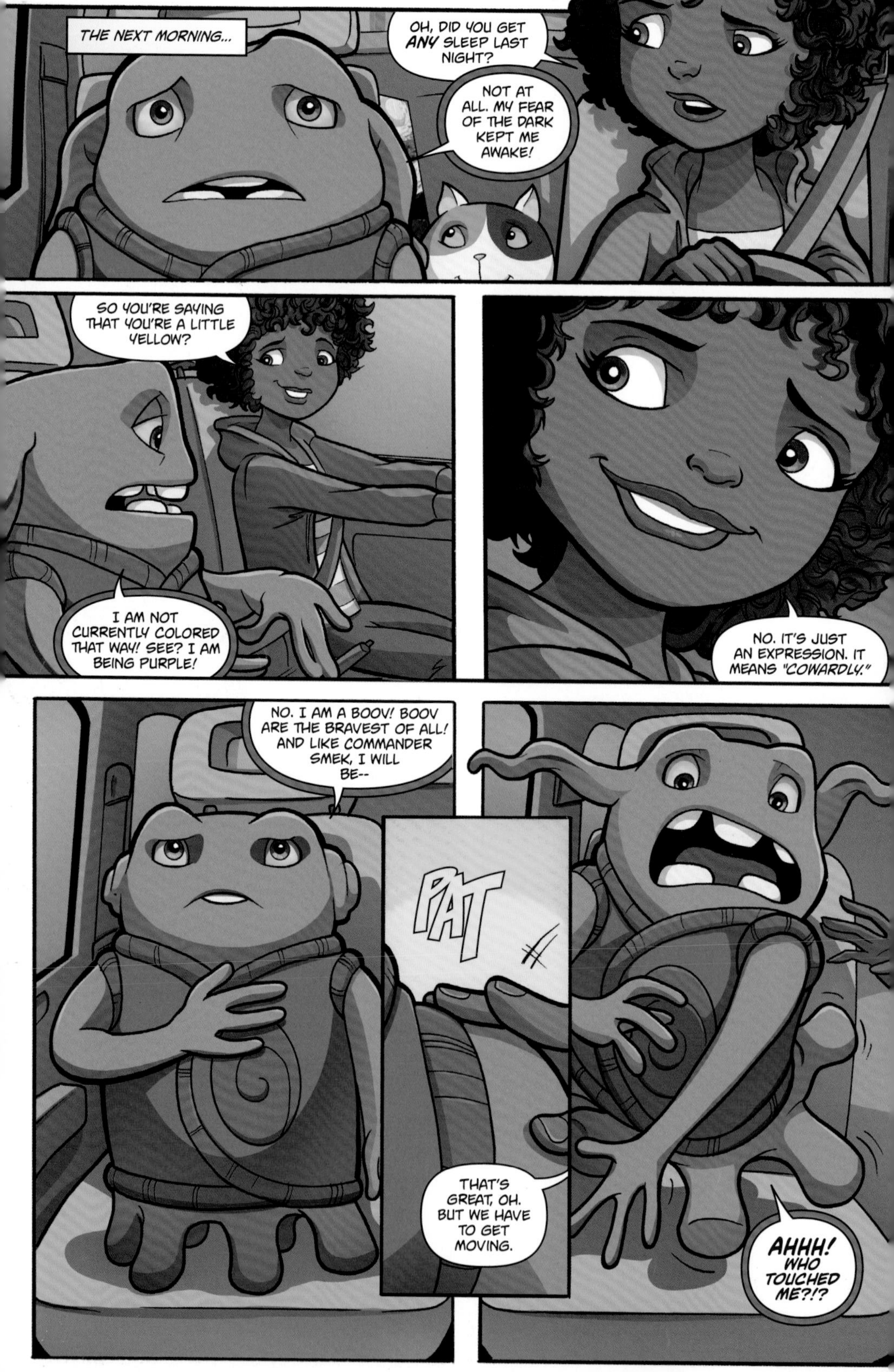
THE NEXT MORNING...
OH, DID YOU GET ANY SLEEP LAST NIGHT?
NOT AT ALL. MY FEAR OF THE DARK KEPT ME AWAKE!
SO YOU'RE SAYING THAT YOU'RE A LITTLE YELLOW?
I AM NOT CURRENTLY COLORED THAT WAY! SEE? I AM BEING PURPLE!
NO. IT'S JUST AN EXPRESSION. IT MEANS "COWARDLY."
NO. I AM A BOOV! BOOV ARE THE BRAVEST OF ALL! AND LIKE COMMANDER SMEK, I WILL BE--
PAT
THAT'S GREAT, OH. BUT WE HAVE TO GET MOVING.
AHHH! WHO TOUCHED ME?!?

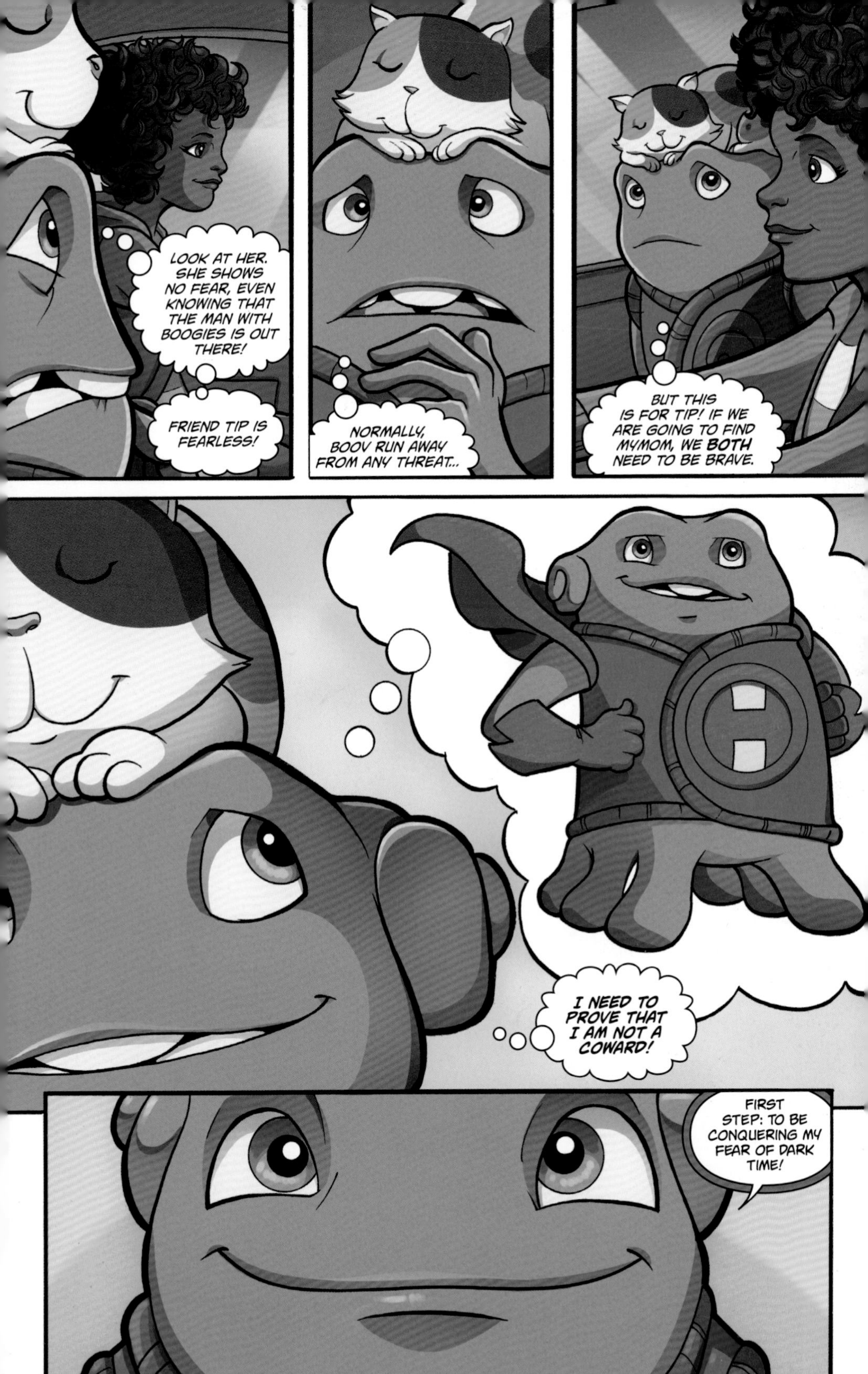
LOOK AT HER. SHE SHOWS NO FEAR, EVEN KNOWING THAT THE MAN WITH BOOGIES IS OUT THERE!
FRIEND TIP IS FEARLESS!
NORMALLY, BOOV RUN AWAY FROM ANY THREAT...
BUT THIS IS FOR TIP! IF WE ARE GOING TO FIND MYMOM, WE BOTH NEED TO BE BRAVE.
I NEED TO PROVE THAT I AM NOT A COWARD!
FIRST STEP: TO BE CONQUERING MY FEAR OF DARK TIME!

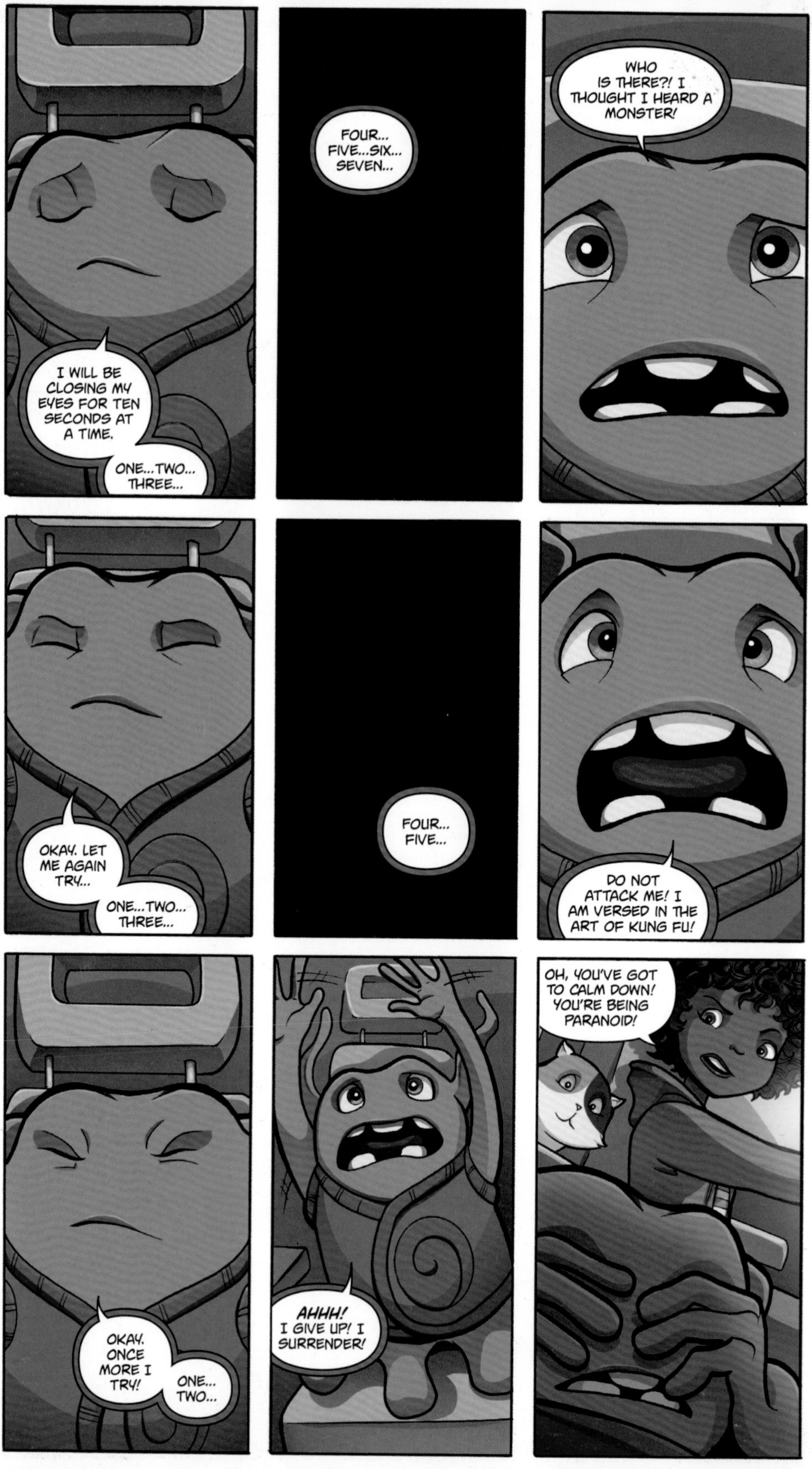
I WILL BE CLOSING MY EYES FOR TEN SECONDS AT A TIME.
ONE...TWO... THREE...
FOUR... FIVE...SIX... SEVEN...
WHO IS THERE?! I THOUGHT I HEARD A MONSTER!
OKAY. LET ME AGAIN TRY...
ONE...TWO... THREE...
FOUR... FIVE...
DO NOT ATTACK ME! I AM VERSED IN THE ART OF KUNG FU!
OKAY. ONCE MORE I TRY!
ONE... TWO...
AHHH! I GIVE UP! I SURRENDER!
OH, YOU'VE GOT TO CALM DOWN! YOU'RE BEING PARANOID!

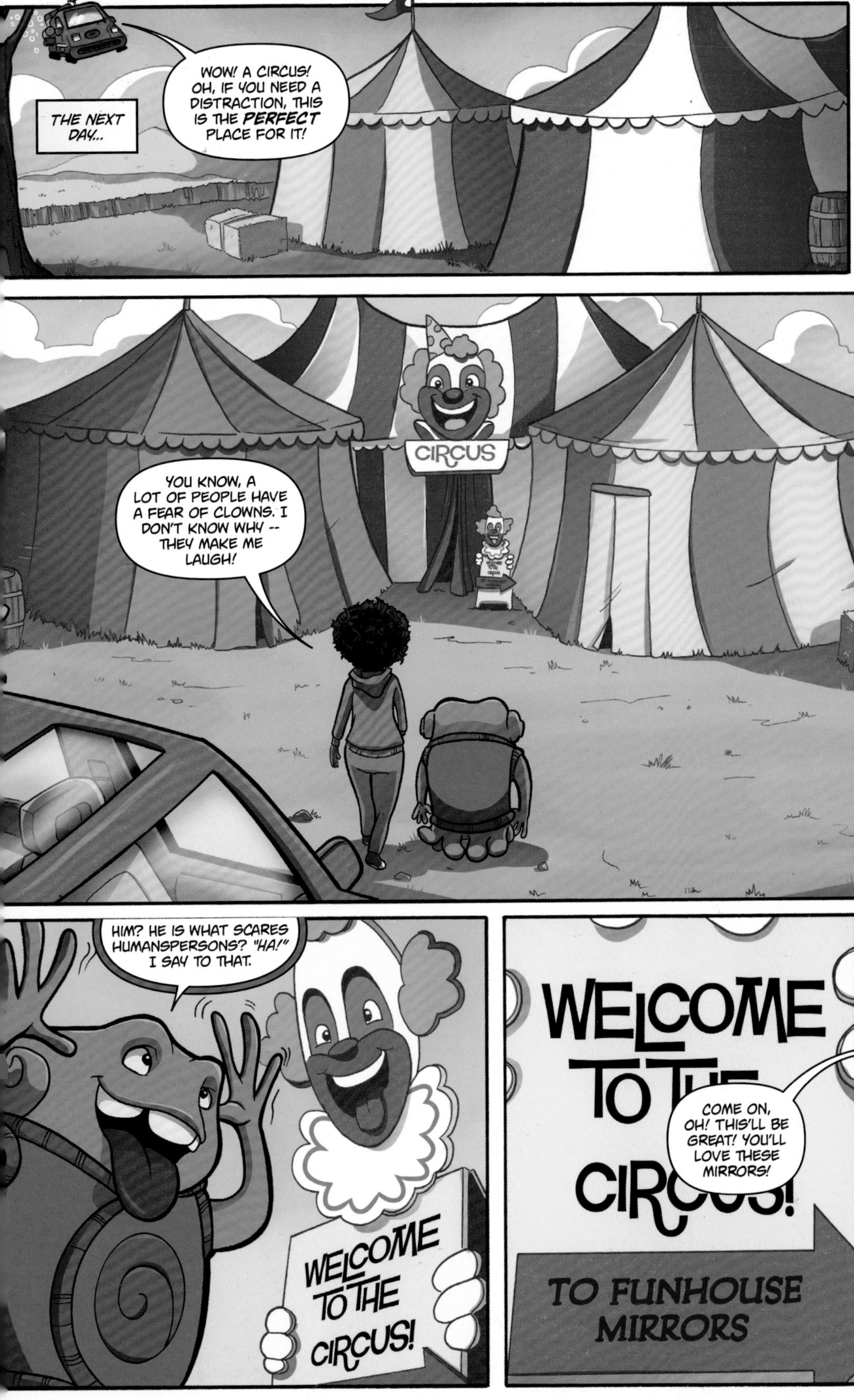
THE NEXT DAY...
WOW! A CIRCUS! OH, IF YOU NEED A DISTRACTION, THIS IS THE PERFECT PLACE FOR IT!
CIRCUS
YOU KNOW, A LOT OF PEOPLE HAVE A FEAR OF CLOWNS. I DON'T KNOW WHY -- THEY MAKE ME LAUGH!
HIM? HE IS WHAT SCARES HUMANSPERSONS? "HA!" I SAY TO THAT.
WELCOME TO THE CIRCUS!
WELCOME
COME ON, OH! THIS'LL BE GREAT! YOU'LL LOVE THESE MIRRORS!
TO FUNHOUSE MIRRORS

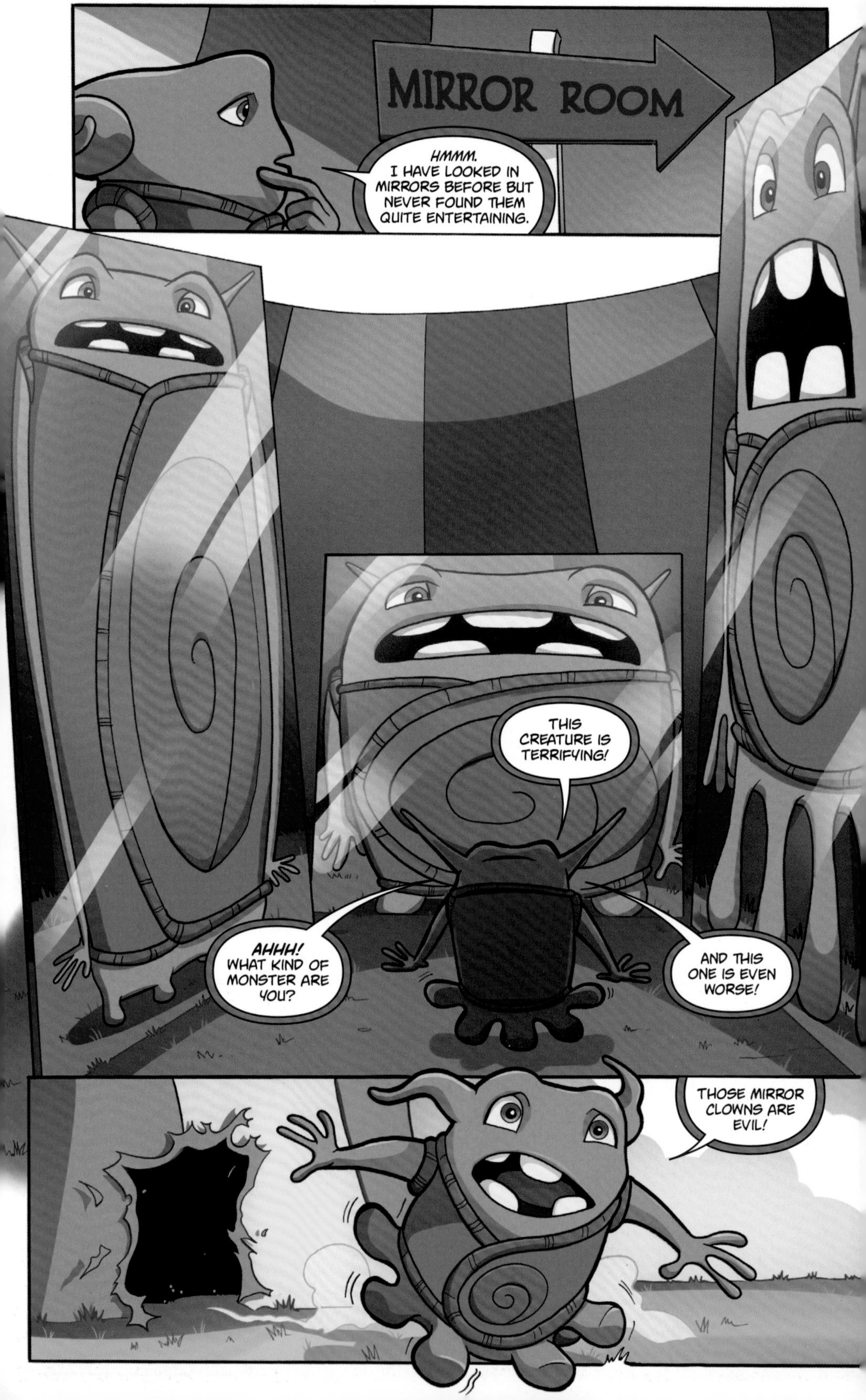
MIRROR ROOM
HMMM. I HAVE LOOKED IN MIRRORS BEFORE BUT NEVER FOUND THEM QUITE ENTERTAINING.
THIS CREATURE IS TERRIFYING!
AHHH! WHAT KIND OF MONSTER ARE YOU?
AND THIS ONE IS EVEN WORSE!
THOSE MIRROR CLOWNS ARE EVIL!

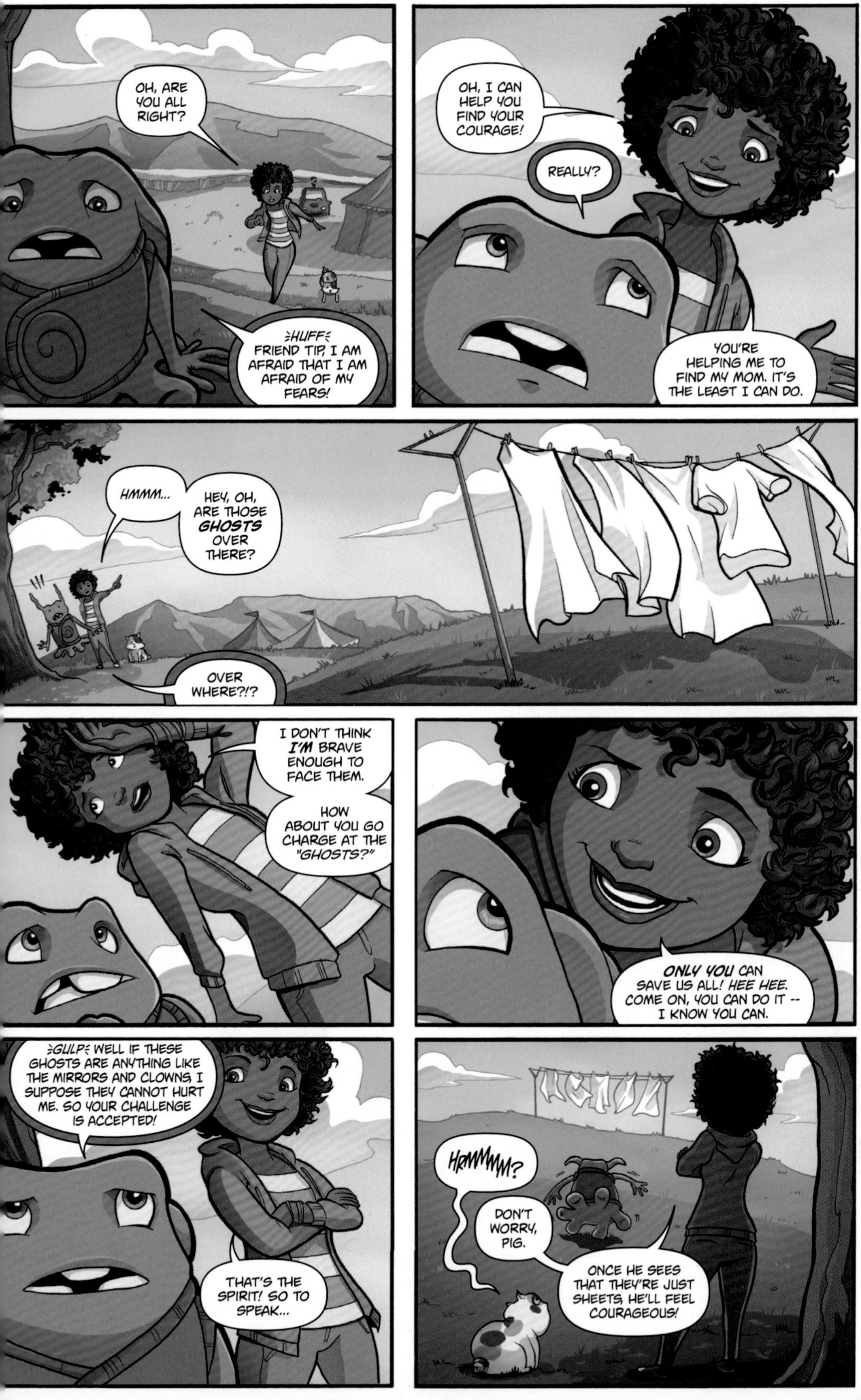
OH, ARE YOU ALL RIGHT?
≡HUFF≡ FRIEND TIP, I AM AFRAID THAT I AM AFRAID OF MY FEARS!
OH, I CAN HELP YOU FIND YOUR COURAGE!
REALLY?
YOU'RE HELPING ME TO FIND MY MOM. IT'S THE LEAST I CAN DO.
HMMM...
HEY, OH, ARE THOSE GHOSTS OVER THERE?
OVER WHERE?!?
I DON'T THINK I'M BRAVE ENOUGH TO FACE THEM.
HOW ABOUT YOU GO CHARGE AT THE "GHOSTS?"
ONLY YOU CAN SAVE US ALL! HEE HEE. COME ON, YOU CAN DO IT -- I KNOW YOU CAN.
≡GULP≡ WELL IF THESE GHOSTS ARE ANYTHING LIKE THE MIRRORS AND CLOWNS, I SUPPOSE THEY CANNOT HURT ME. SO YOUR CHALLENGE IS ACCEPTED!
THAT'S THE SPIRIT! SO TO SPEAK...
HRMMMM?
DON'T WORRY, PIG.
ONCE HE SEES THAT THEY'RE JUST SHEETS, HE'LL FEEL COURAGEOUS!

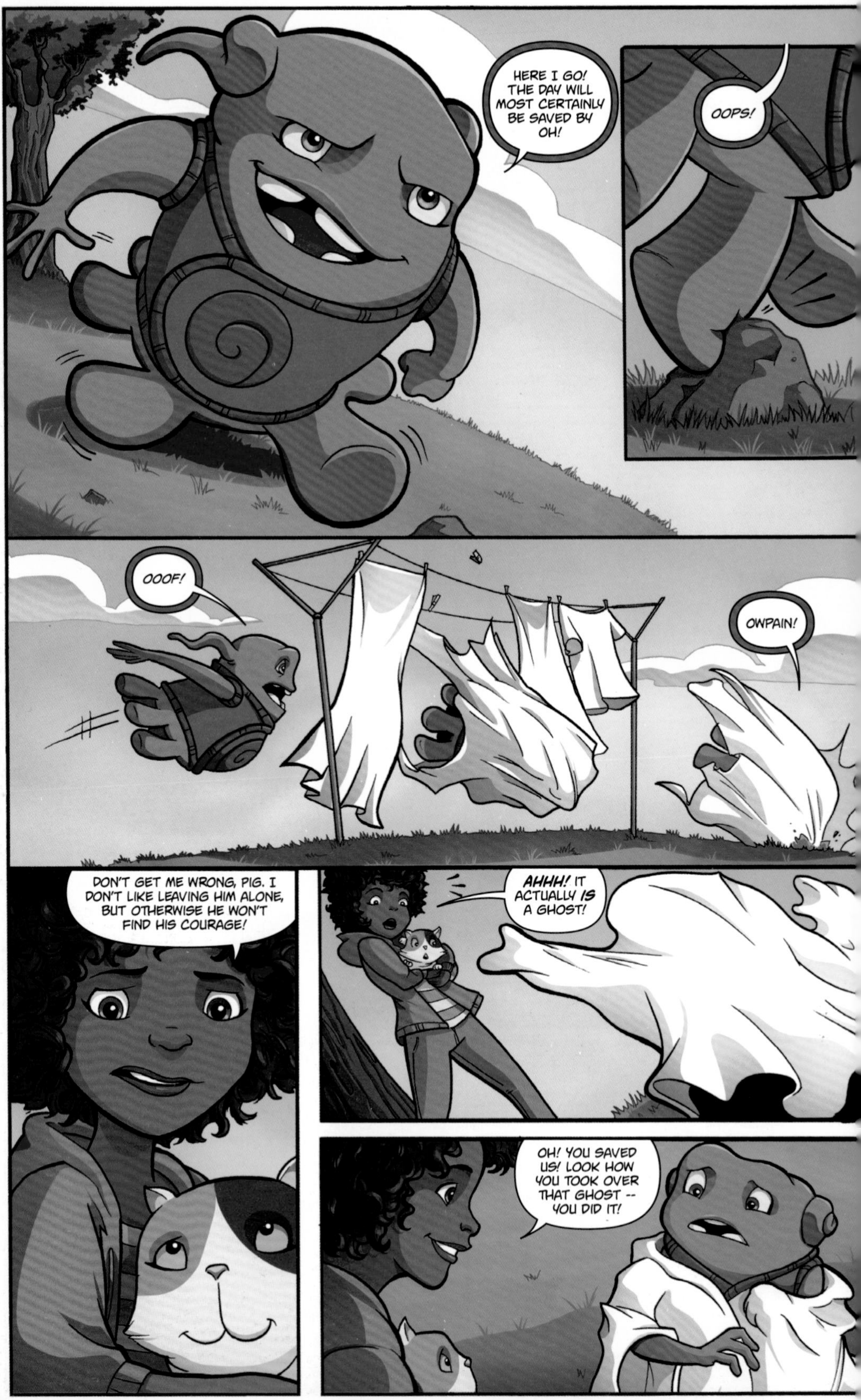
HERE I GO! THE DAY WILL MOST CERTAINLY BE SAVED BY OH!
OOPS!
OOOF!
OWPAIN!
DON'T GET ME WRONG, PIG. I DON'T LIKE LEAVING HIM ALONE, BUT OTHERWISE HE WON'T FIND HIS COURAGE!
AHHH! IT ACTUALLY IS A GHOST!
OH! YOU SAVED US! LOOK HOW YOU TOOK OVER THAT GHOST -- YOU DID IT!

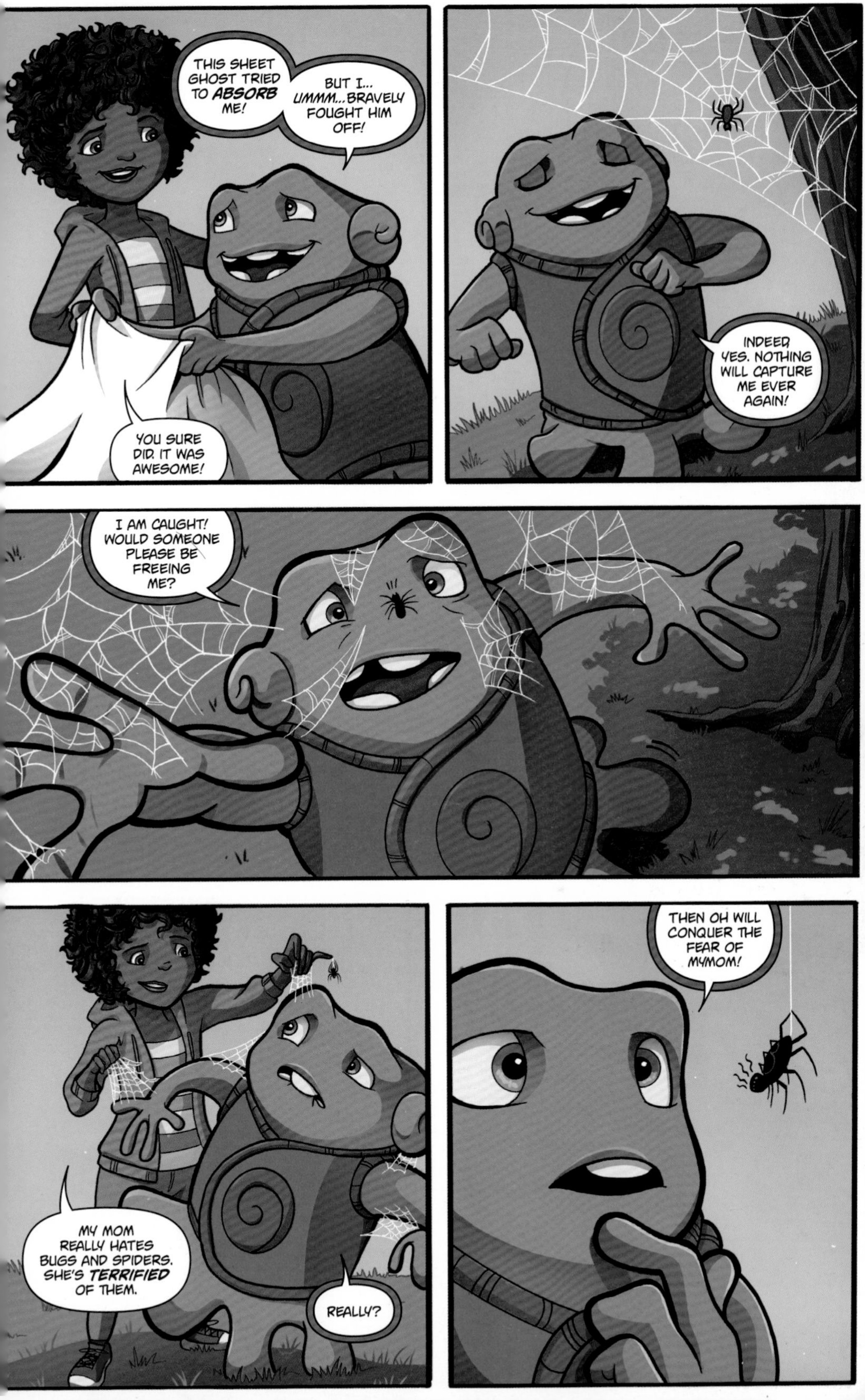
THIS SHEET GHOST TRIED TO **ABSORB** ME!
BUT I... *UMMM*...BRAVELY FOUGHT HIM OFF!
YOU SURE DID. IT WAS AWESOME!
INDEED, YES. NOTHING WILL CAPTURE ME EVER AGAIN!
I AM CAUGHT! WOULD SOMEONE PLEASE BE FREEING ME?
MY MOM REALLY HATES BUGS AND SPIDERS. SHE'S **TERRIFIED** OF THEM.
REALLY?
THEN OH WILL CONQUER THE FEAR OF MYMOM!

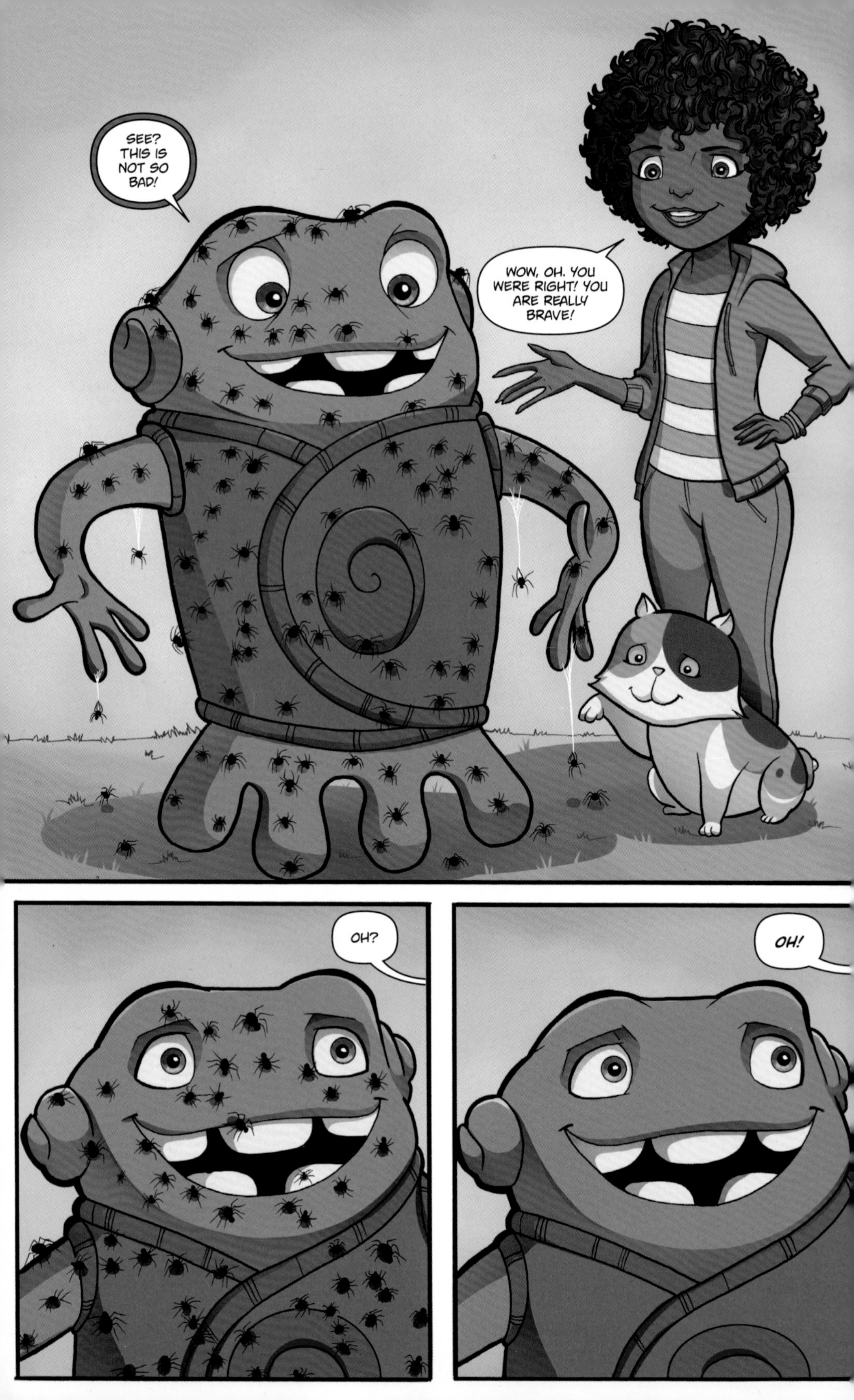
SEE? THIS IS NOT SO BAD!
WOW, OH. YOU WERE RIGHT! YOU ARE REALLY BRAVE!
OH?
OH!

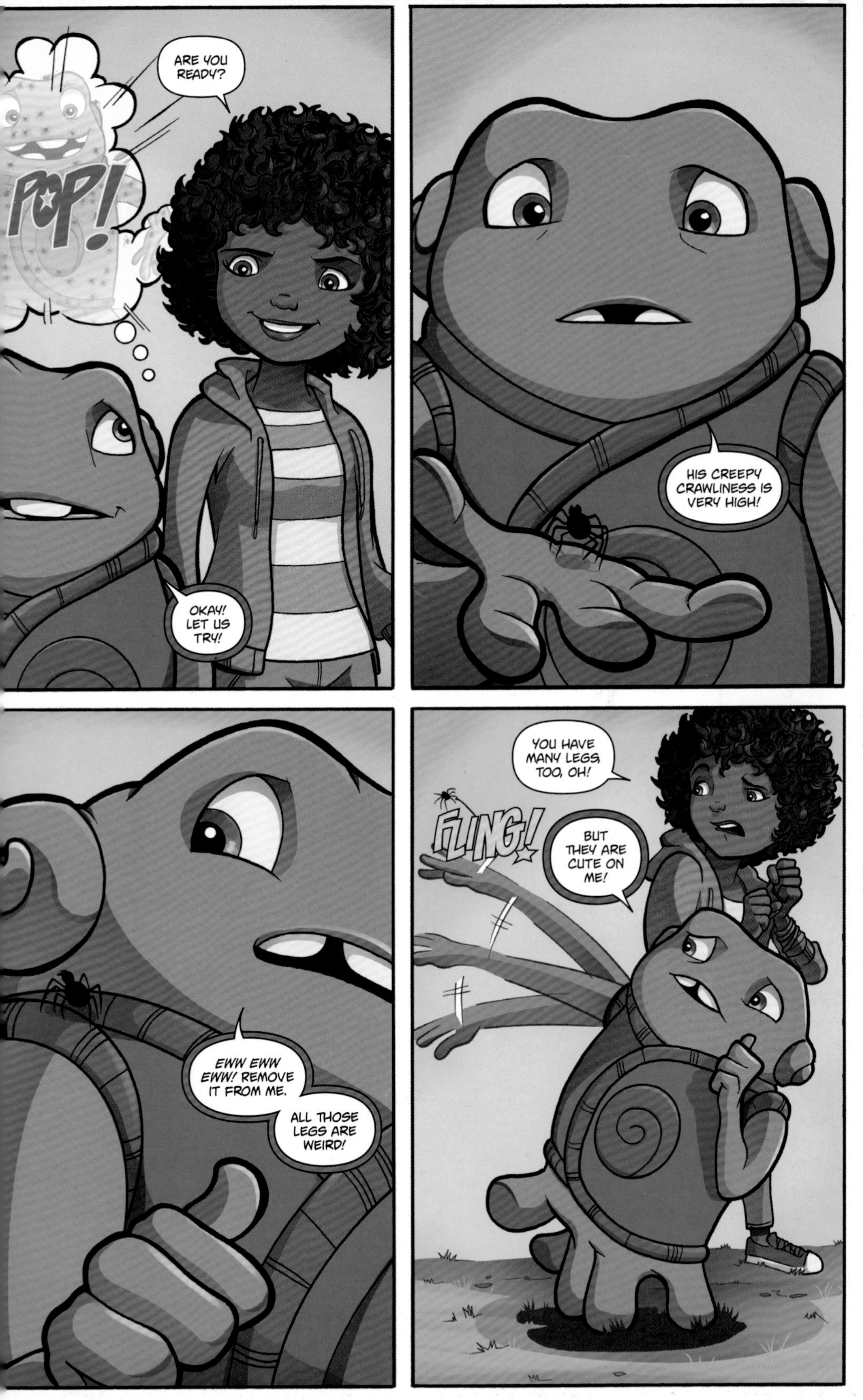
POP!
ARE YOU READY?
OKAY! LET US TRY!
HIS CREEPY CRAWLINESS IS VERY HIGH!
EWW EWW EWW! REMOVE IT FROM ME.
ALL THOSE LEGS ARE WEIRD!
YOU HAVE MANY LEGS, TOO, OH!
FLING!
BUT THEY ARE CUTE ON ME!

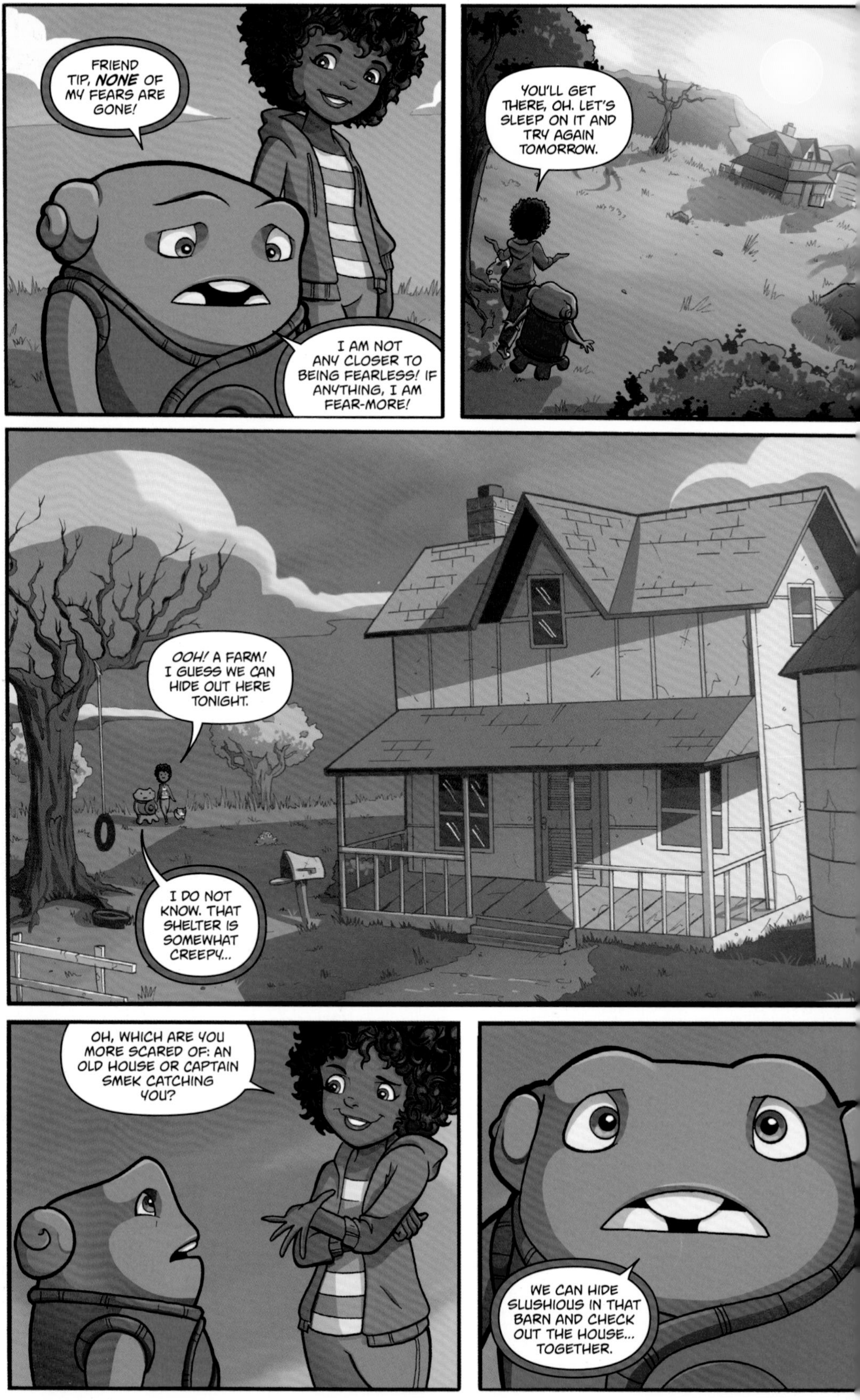
FRIEND TIP, NONE OF MY FEARS ARE GONE!
I AM NOT ANY CLOSER TO BEING FEARLESS! IF ANYTHING, I AM FEAR-MORE!
YOU'LL GET THERE, OH. LET'S SLEEP ON IT AND TRY AGAIN TOMORROW.
OOH! A FARM! I GUESS WE CAN HIDE OUT HERE TONIGHT.
I DO NOT KNOW. THAT SHELTER IS SOMEWHAT CREEPY...
OH, WHICH ARE YOU MORE SCARED OF: AN OLD HOUSE OR CAPTAIN SMEK CATCHING YOU?
WE CAN HIDE SLUSHIOUS IN THAT BARN AND CHECK OUT THE HOUSE... TOGETHER.

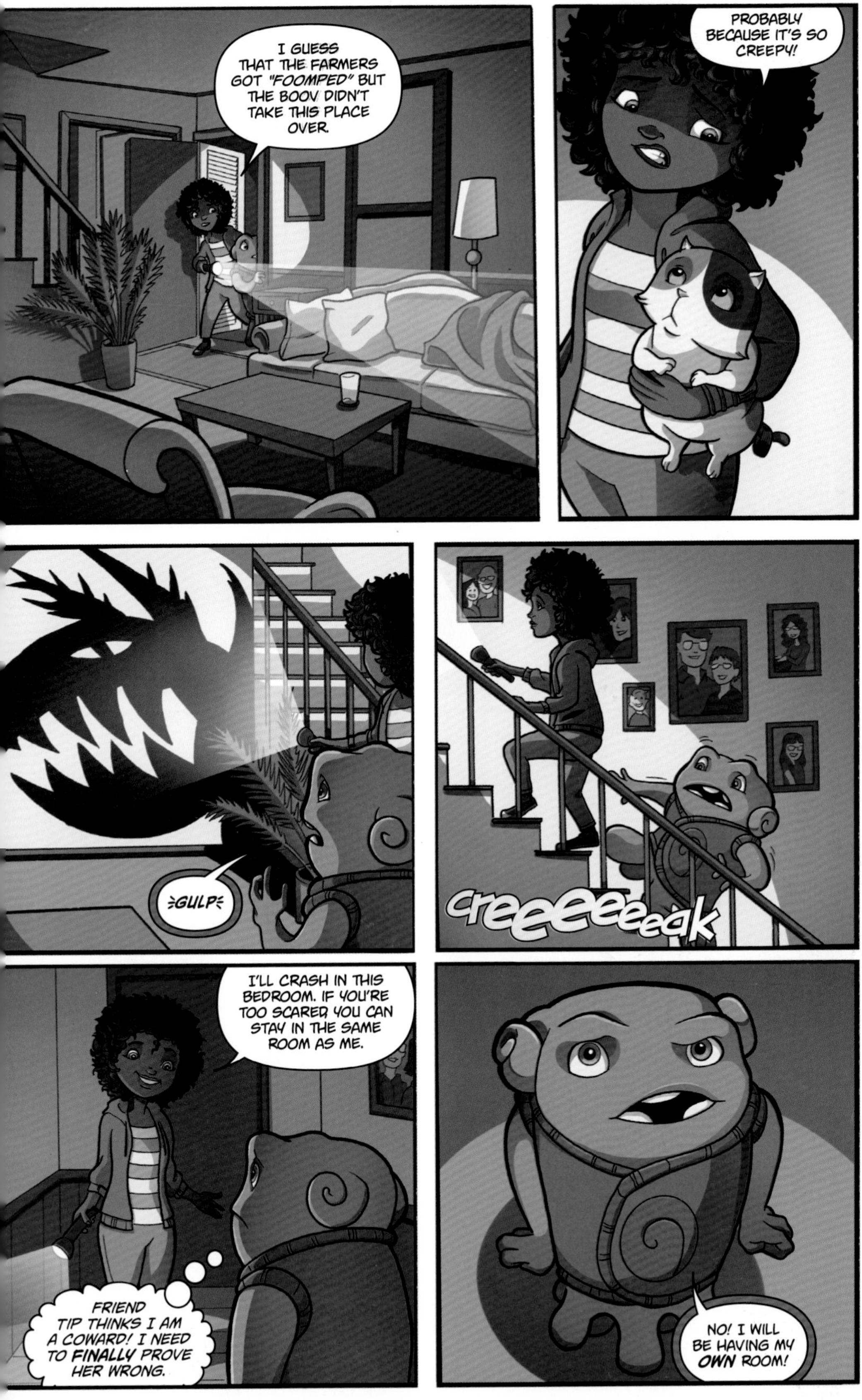
I GUESS THAT THE FARMERS GOT "FOOMPED" BUT THE BOOV DIDN'T TAKE THIS PLACE OVER.
PROBABLY BECAUSE IT'S SO CREEPY!
GULP
creeeeeeak
I'LL CRASH IN THIS BEDROOM. IF YOU'RE TOO SCARED YOU CAN STAY IN THE SAME ROOM AS ME.
FRIEND TIP THINKS I AM A COWARD! I NEED TO FINALLY PROVE HER WRONG.
NO! I WILL BE HAVING MY OWN ROOM!

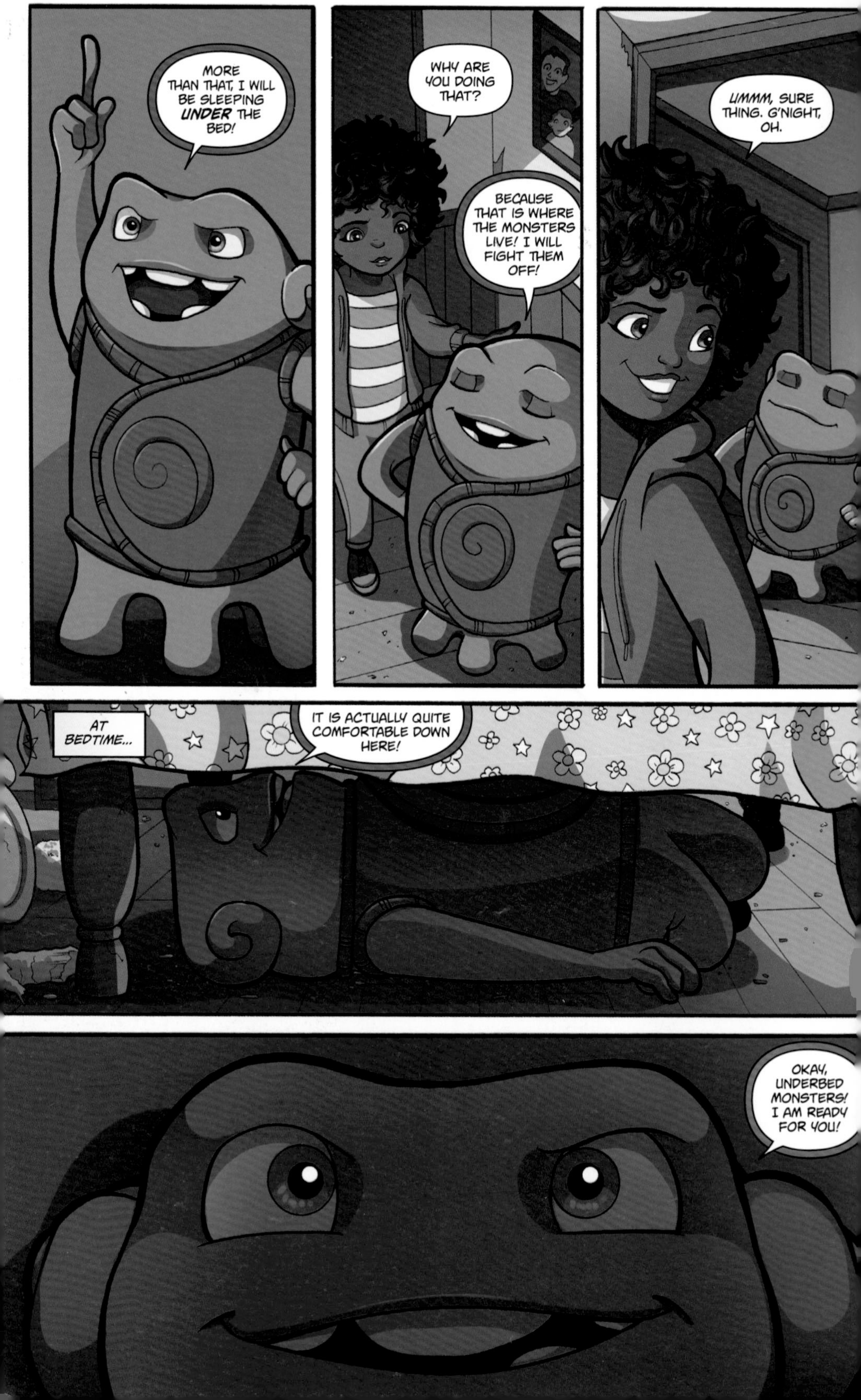

MORE THAN THAT, I WILL BE SLEEPING UNDER THE BED!
WHY ARE YOU DOING THAT?
BECAUSE THAT IS WHERE THE MONSTERS LIVE! I WILL FIGHT THEM OFF!
UMMM, SURE THING. G'NIGHT, OH.
AT BEDTIME...
IT IS ACTUALLY QUITE COMFORTABLE DOWN HERE!
OKAY, UNDERBED MONSTERS! I AM READY FOR YOU!

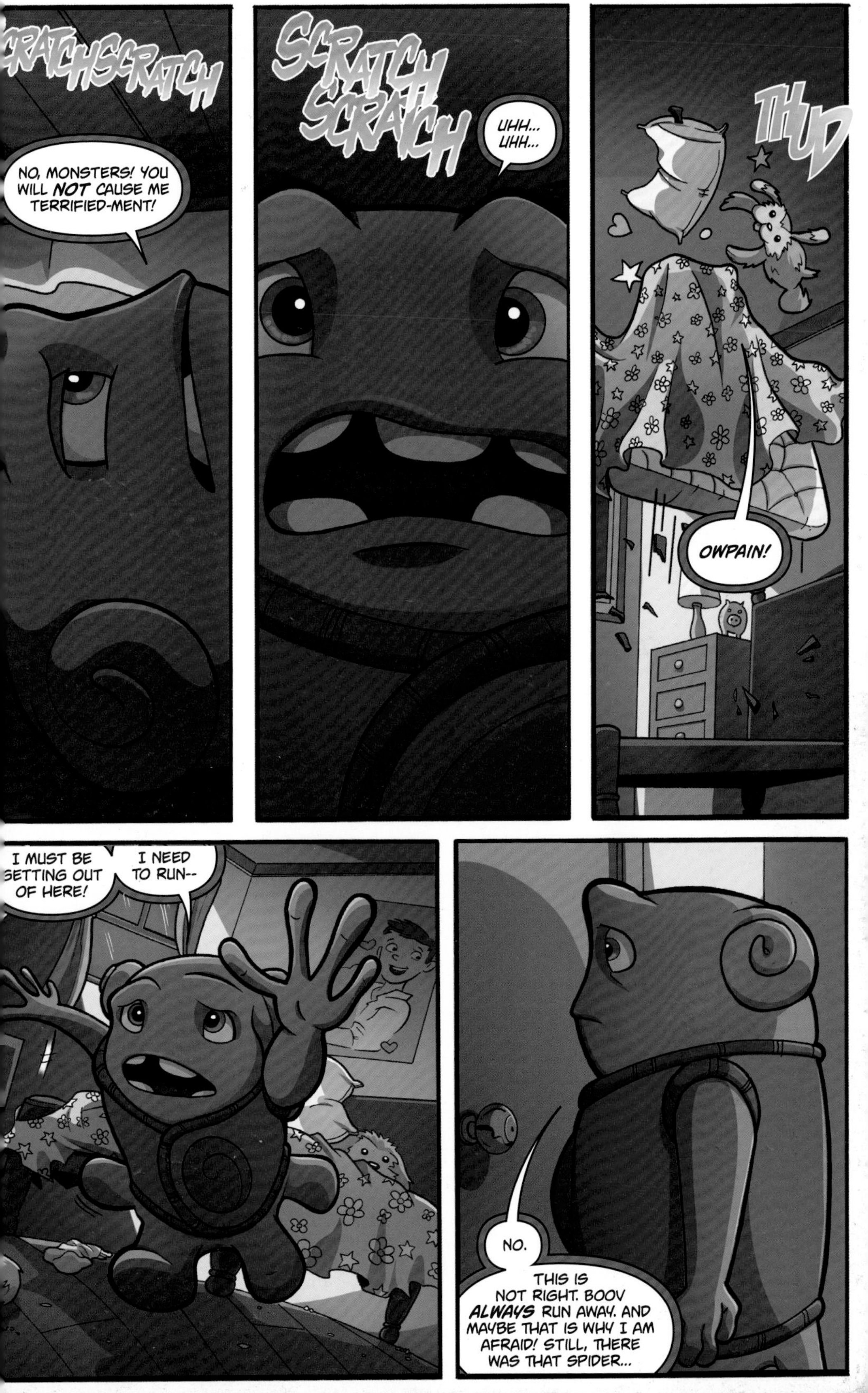
SCRATCHSCRATCH
NO, MONSTERS! YOU WILL NOT CAUSE ME TERRIFIED-MENT!
SCRATCH SCRATCH
UHH... UHH...
THUD
OWPAIN!
I MUST BE GETTING OUT OF HERE!
I NEED TO RUN--
NO.
THIS IS NOT RIGHT. BOOV ALWAYS RUN AWAY. AND MAYBE THAT IS WHY I AM AFRAID! STILL, THERE WAS THAT SPIDER...

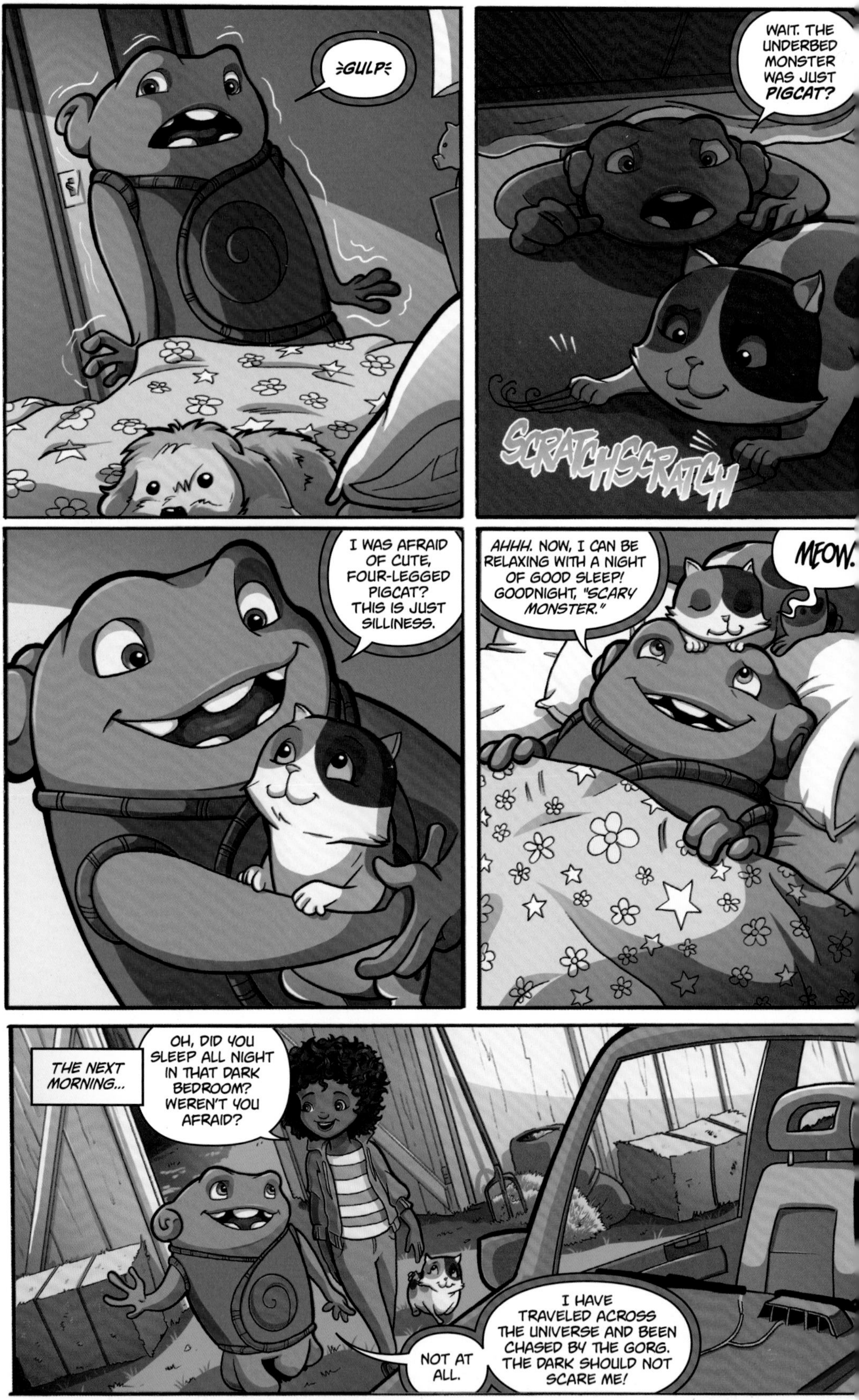
GULP
WAIT. THE UNDERBED MONSTER WAS JUST PIGCAT?
SCRATCHSCRATCH
I WAS AFRAID OF CUTE, FOUR-LEGGED PIGCAT? THIS IS JUST SILLINESS.
AHHH. NOW, I CAN BE RELAXING WITH A NIGHT OF GOOD SLEEP! GOODNIGHT, "SCARY MONSTER."
MEOW.
THE NEXT MORNING...
OH, DID YOU SLEEP ALL NIGHT IN THAT DARK BEDROOM? WEREN'T YOU AFRAID?
NOT AT ALL.
I HAVE TRAVELED ACROSS THE UNIVERSE AND BEEN CHASED BY THE GORG. THE DARK SHOULD NOT SCARE ME!

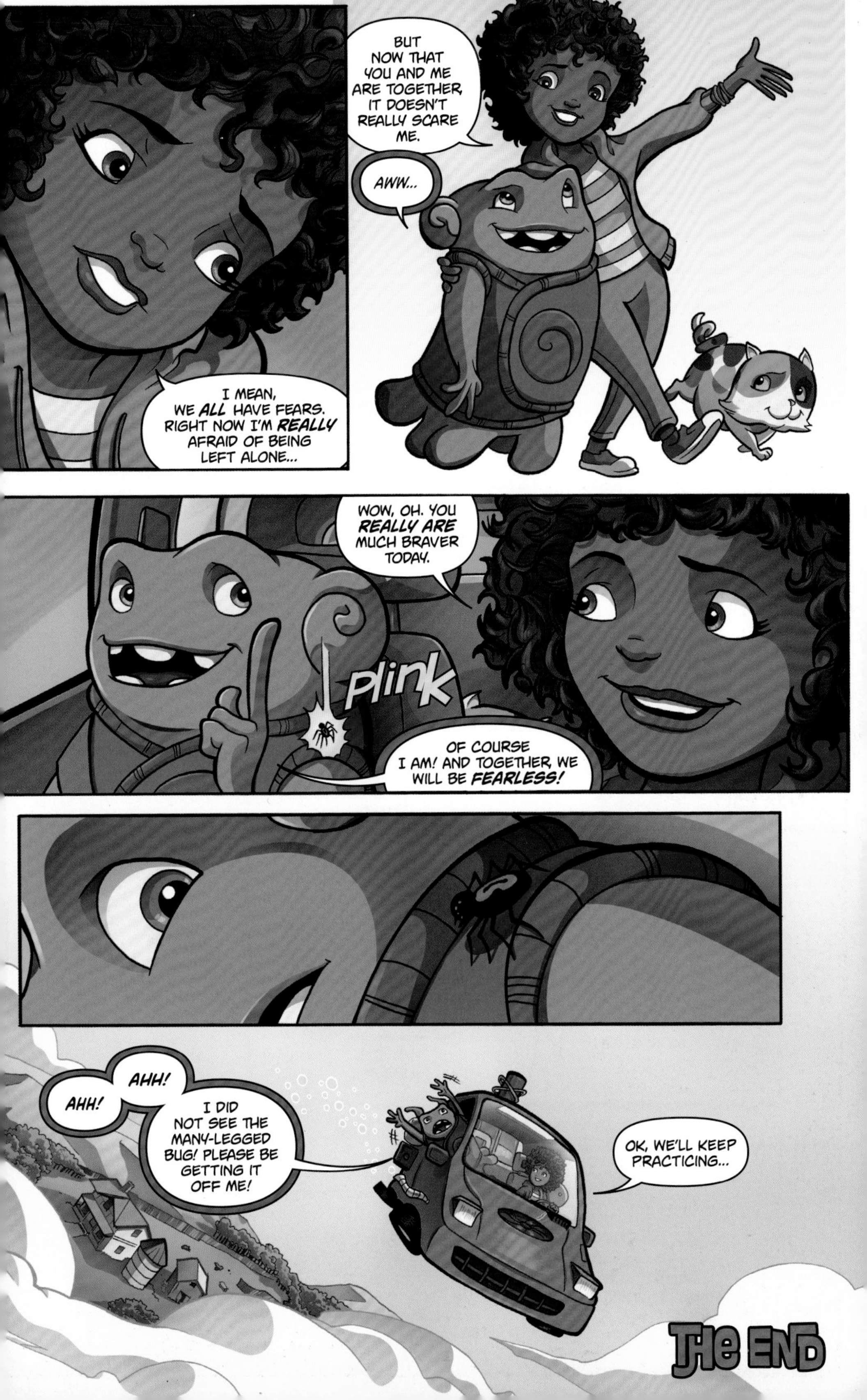
I MEAN, WE ALL HAVE FEARS. RIGHT NOW I'M REALLY AFRAID OF BEING LEFT ALONE...
BUT NOW THAT YOU AND ME ARE TOGETHER, IT DOESN'T REALLY SCARE ME.
AWW...
WOW, OH. YOU REALLY ARE MUCH BRAVER TODAY.
plink
OF COURSE I AM! AND TOGETHER, WE WILL BE FEARLESS!
AHH!
AHH!
I DID NOT SEE THE MANY-LEGGED BUG! PLEASE BE GETTING IT OFF ME!
OK, WE'LL KEEP PRACTICING...
THE END

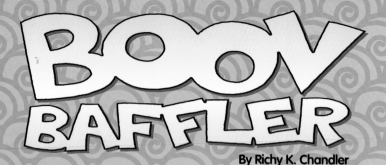

BOOV BAFFLER

By Richy K. Chandler

The Boov are partying on the moon! Can you find Oh, Tip, Pig, Kyle and Captain Smek in this big picture? You'll need to find Oh's exact pose – he's looking like the picture here on the right… (And don't worry, Tip & Pig are wearing li'l space helmets!)

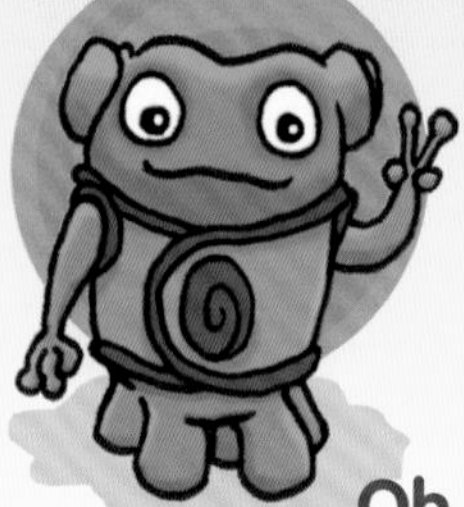

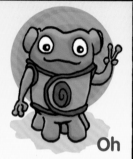

Oh

HAVE YOU SEEN US?

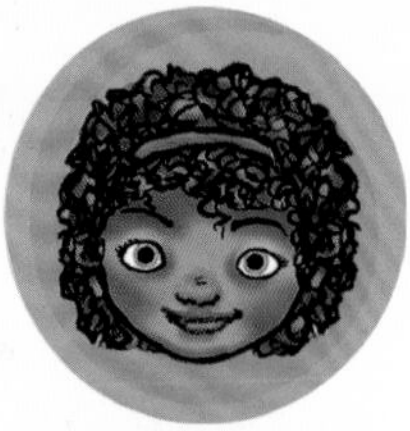

Tip

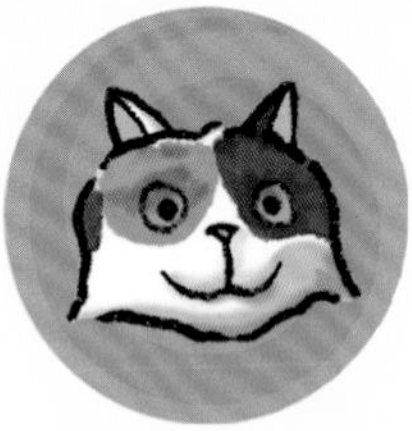

Pig

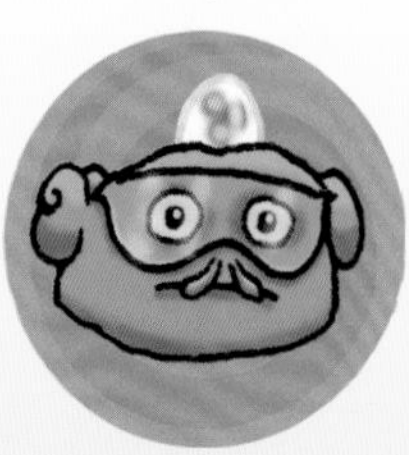

Kyle

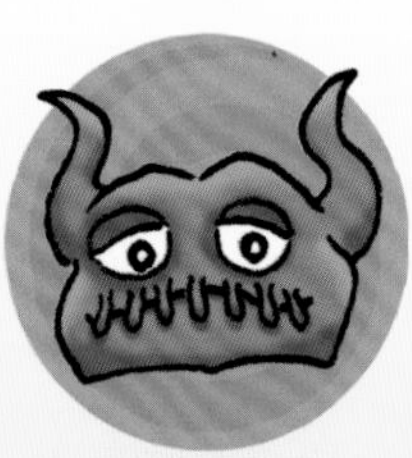

Captain Smek

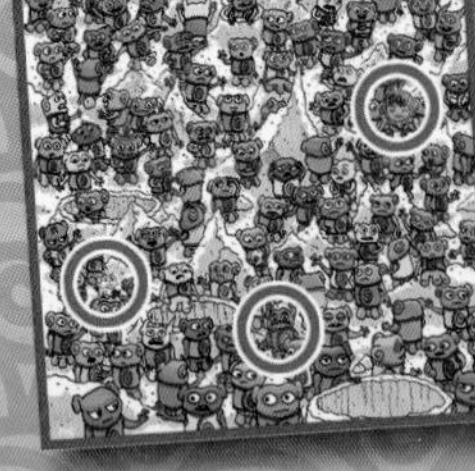

ANSWERS

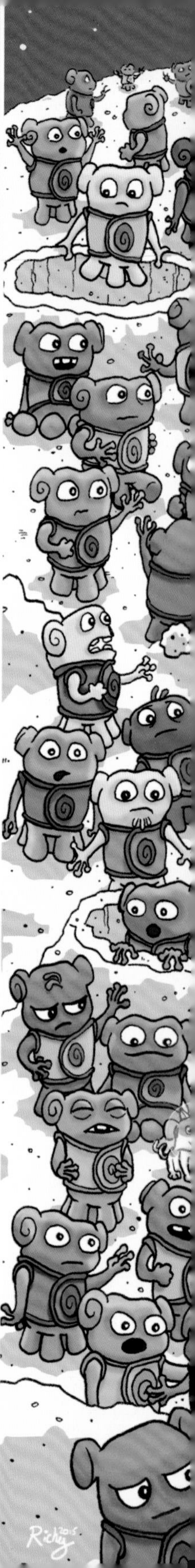
Richy 2015

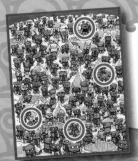

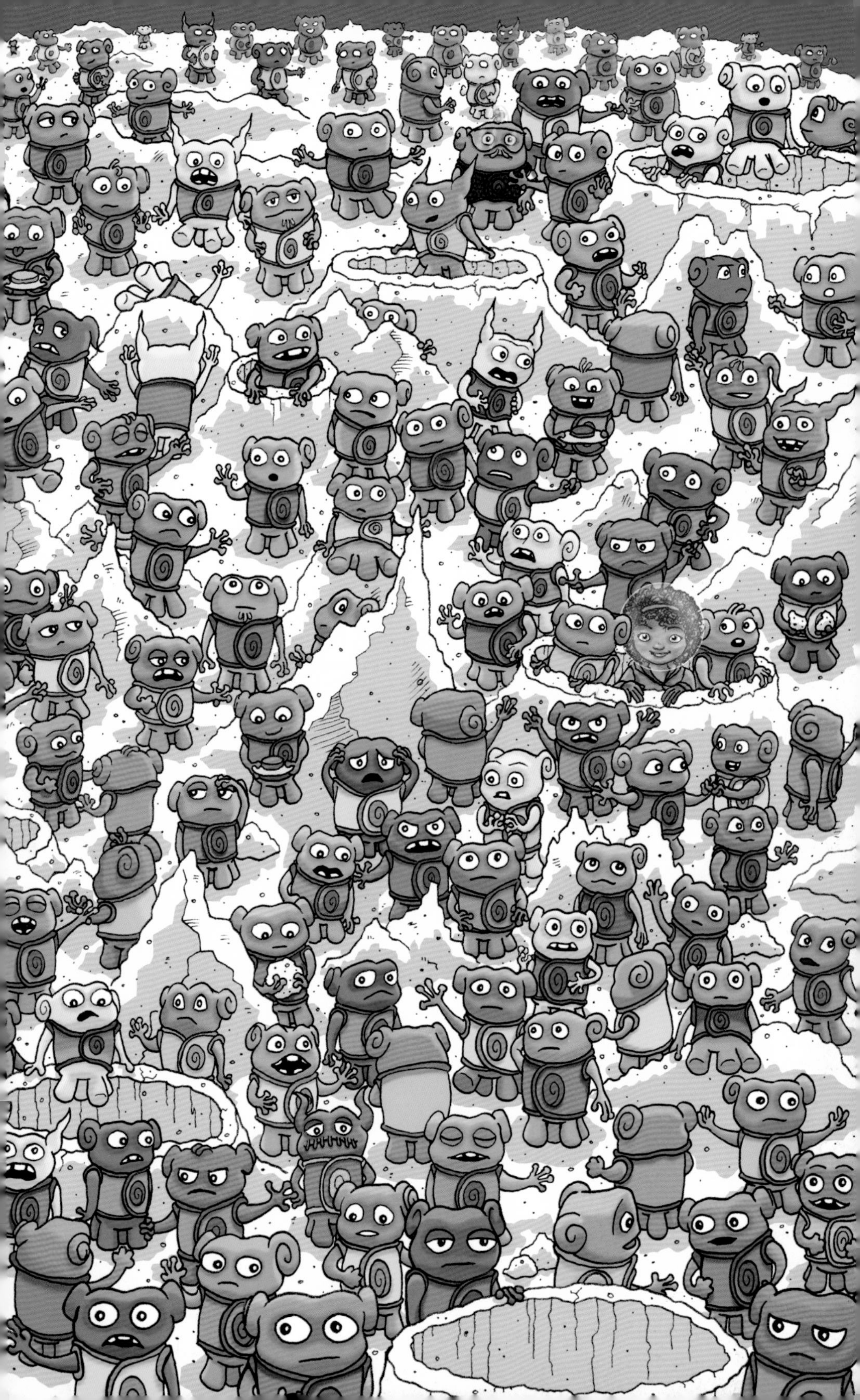

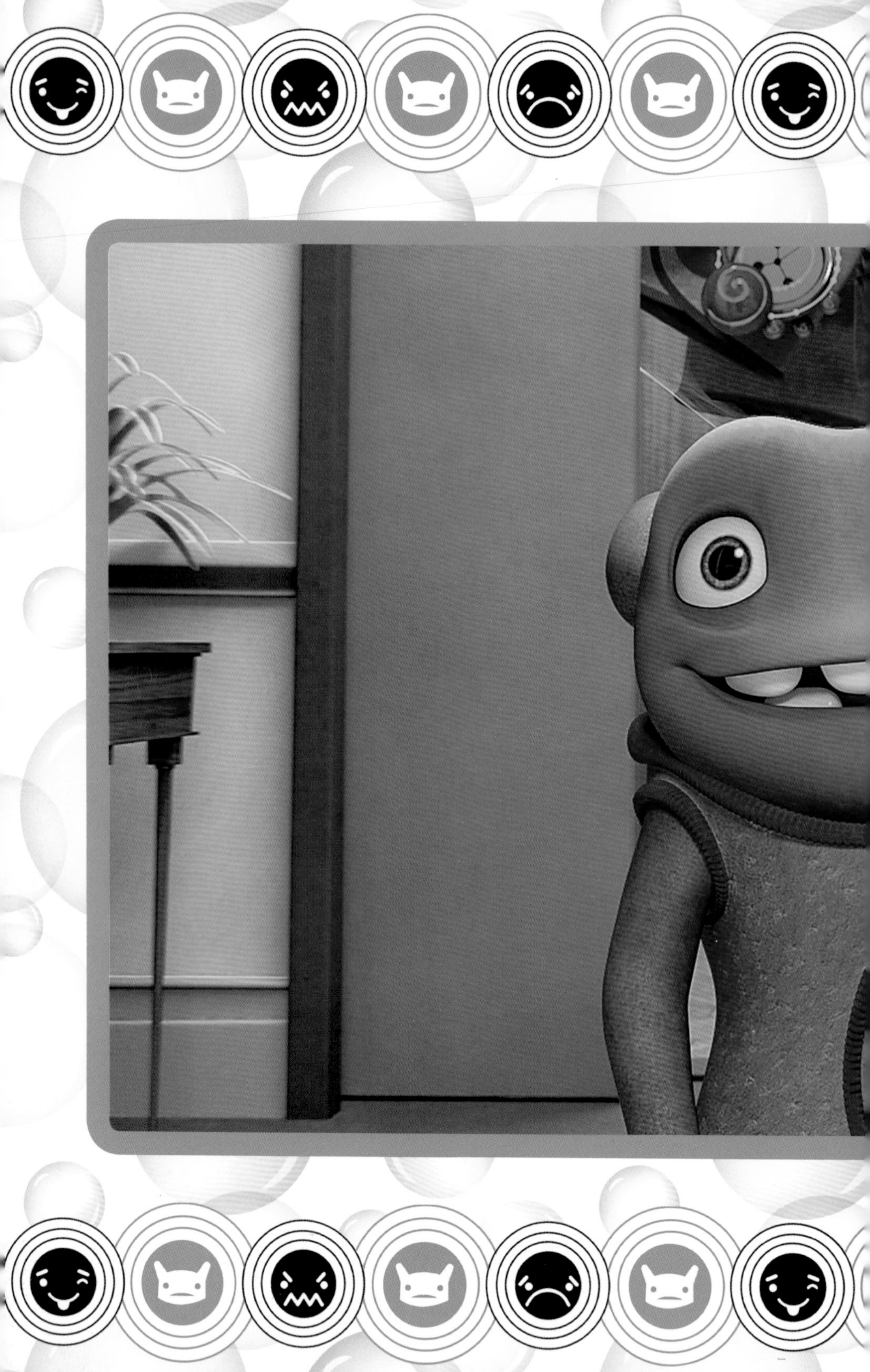

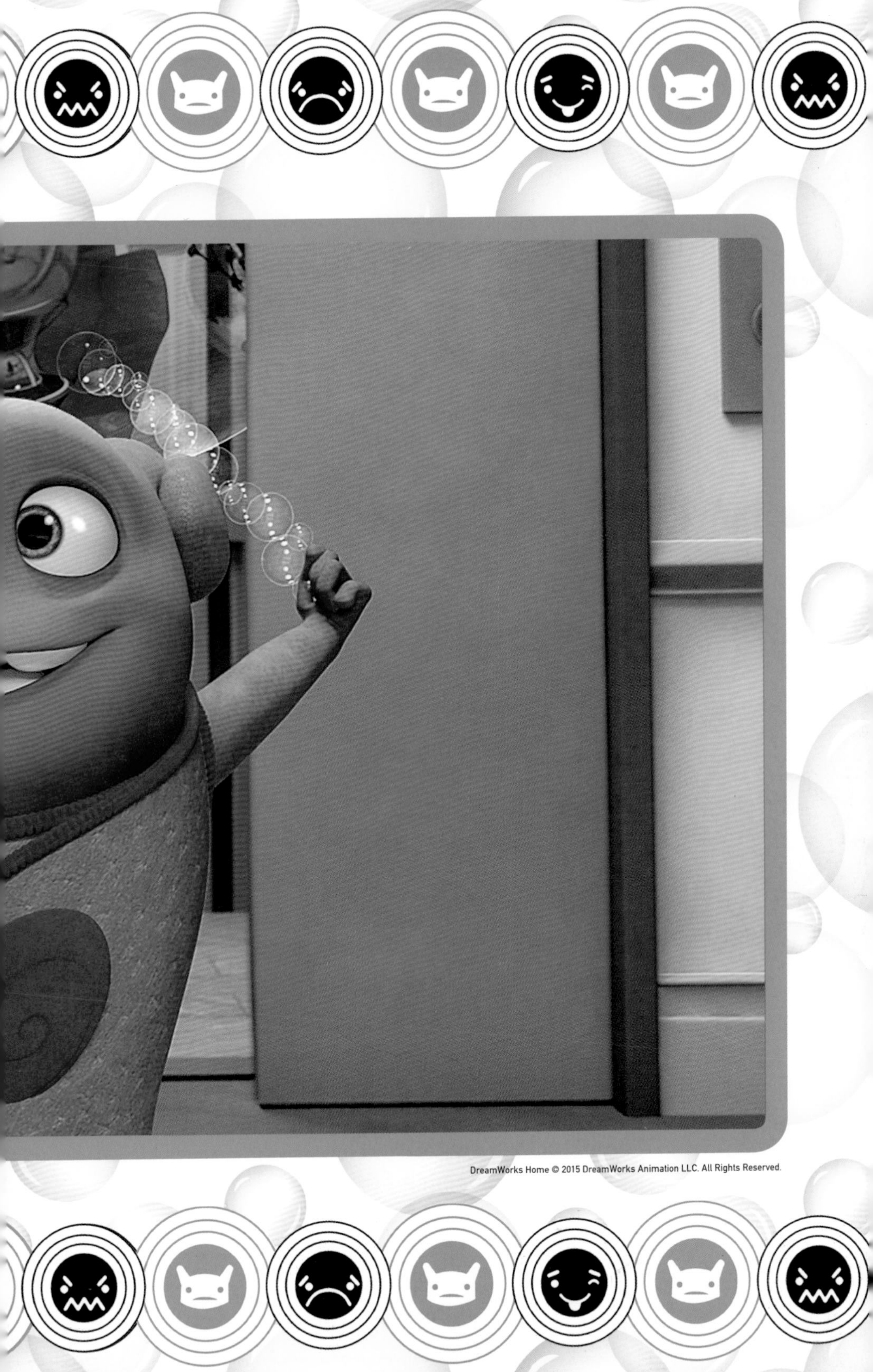

PENGUINS OF MADAGASCAR GRAPHIC NOVEL COLLECTION

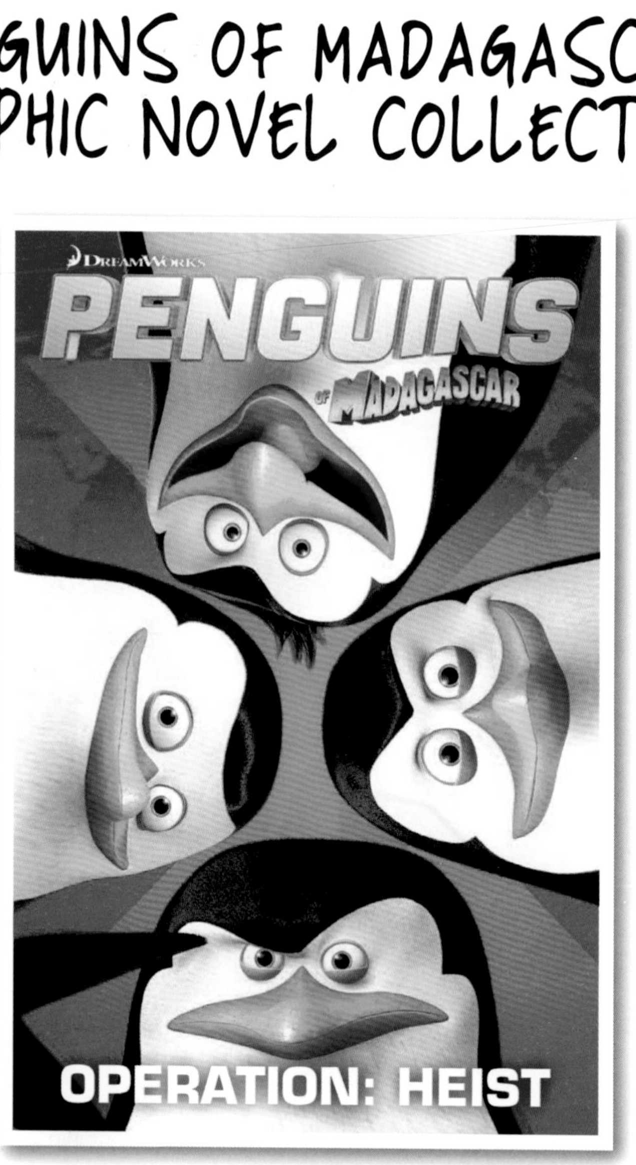
DreamWorks
PENGUINS
OF MADAGASCAR
OPERATION: HEIST

AWESOME COMIC STRIP ANTICS FROM THE *PENGUINS OF MADAGASCAR!*

You've seen them in their own brilliant movie, now read their hilarious comic strips in this brand new collection. In 'Big Top,' the penguins' circus gets a new recruit – the mysterious Claude the Clown… And then in 'Operation: Heist,' arch-villain Clepto the Magpie is on the loose, and he brainwashes Rico into doing his dirty work!

VOLUME 2 ON SALE NOW!

WWW.TITAN-COMICS.COM

TITAN COMICS

DREAMWORKS ANIMATION SKG

KUNG FU PANDA
GRAPHIC NOVEL COLLECTION

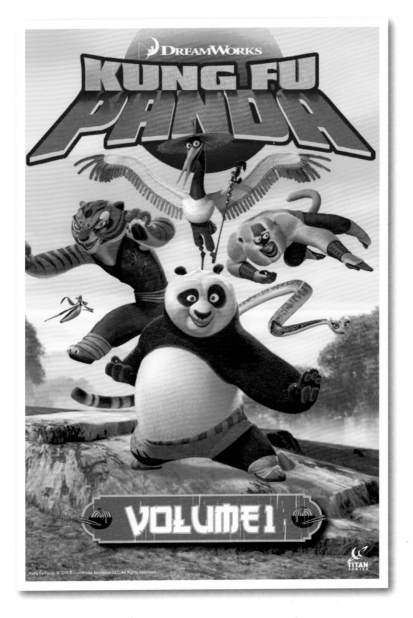

VOLUME 1 COMING SOON!
WWW.TITAN-COMICS.COM

DREAMWORKS DRAGONS: RIDERS OF BERK

Titan Comics presents the most exciting *DreamWorks Dragons: Riders of Berk* adventure yet, written by Simon Furman (*Transformers, Matt Hatter Chronicles*) with incredible art by rising star Iwan Nazif!

During a routine training exercise, Hiccup and his friends discover a huge, mysterious cave in a forest near Berk... meanwhile, Stoick investigates the disappearance of a number of fishing vessels and bumps into an old enemy!

VOLUME 6 ON SALE NOW!

VOLUMES 1 TO 5 ALSO AVAILABLE ONLINE AND IN ALL GOOD BOOKSTORES!

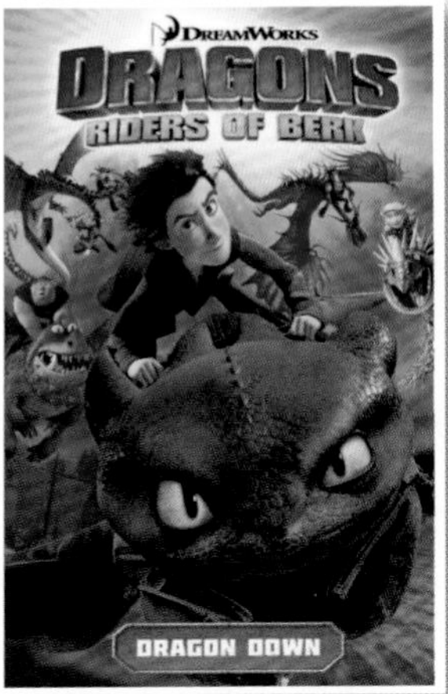
DreamWorks
DRAGONS
RIDERS OF BERK
DRAGON DOWN

VOLUME 1

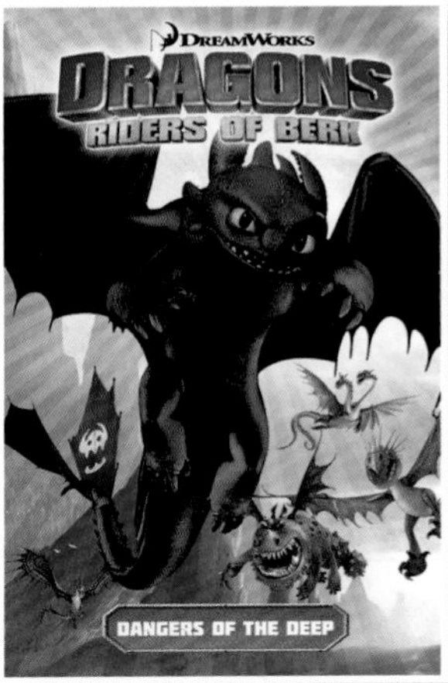
DreamWorks
DRAGONS
RIDERS OF BERK
DANGERS OF THE DEEP

VOLUME 2

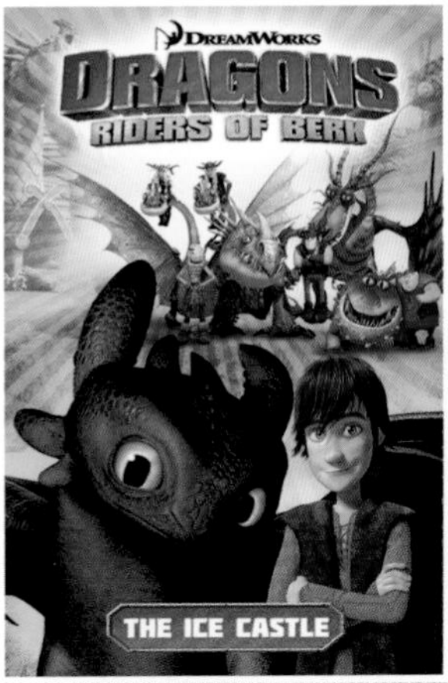
DreamWorks
DRAGONS
RIDERS OF BERK
THE ICE CASTLE

VOLUME 3

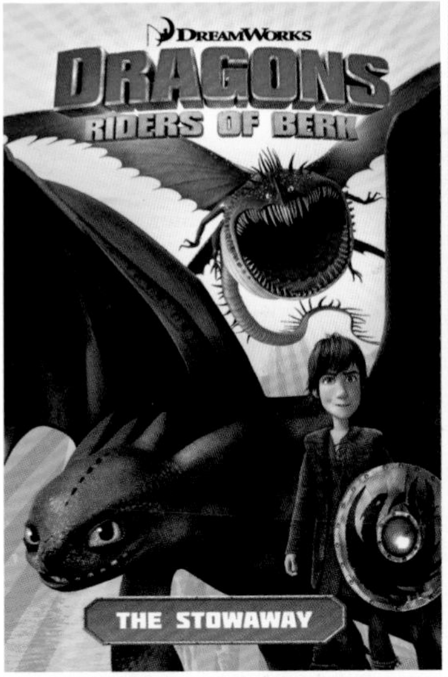
DreamWorks
DRAGONS
RIDERS OF BERK
THE STOWAWAY

VOLUME 4

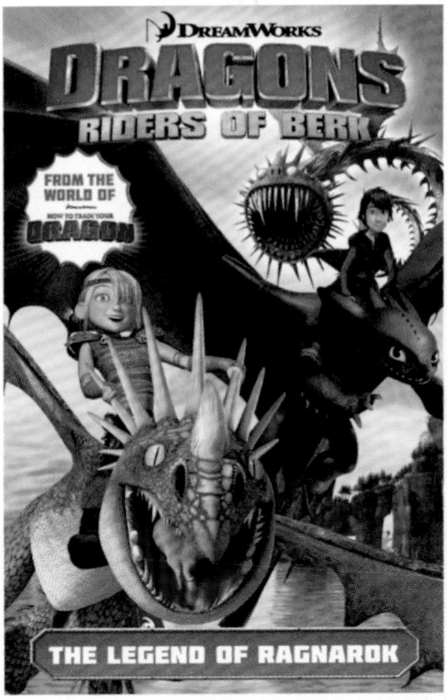
DreamWorks
DRAGONS
RIDERS OF BERK
FROM THE WORLD OF
DRAGON
THE LEGEND OF RAGNAROK

VOLUME 5

WWW.TITAN-COMICS.COM

DreamWorks Animation SKG

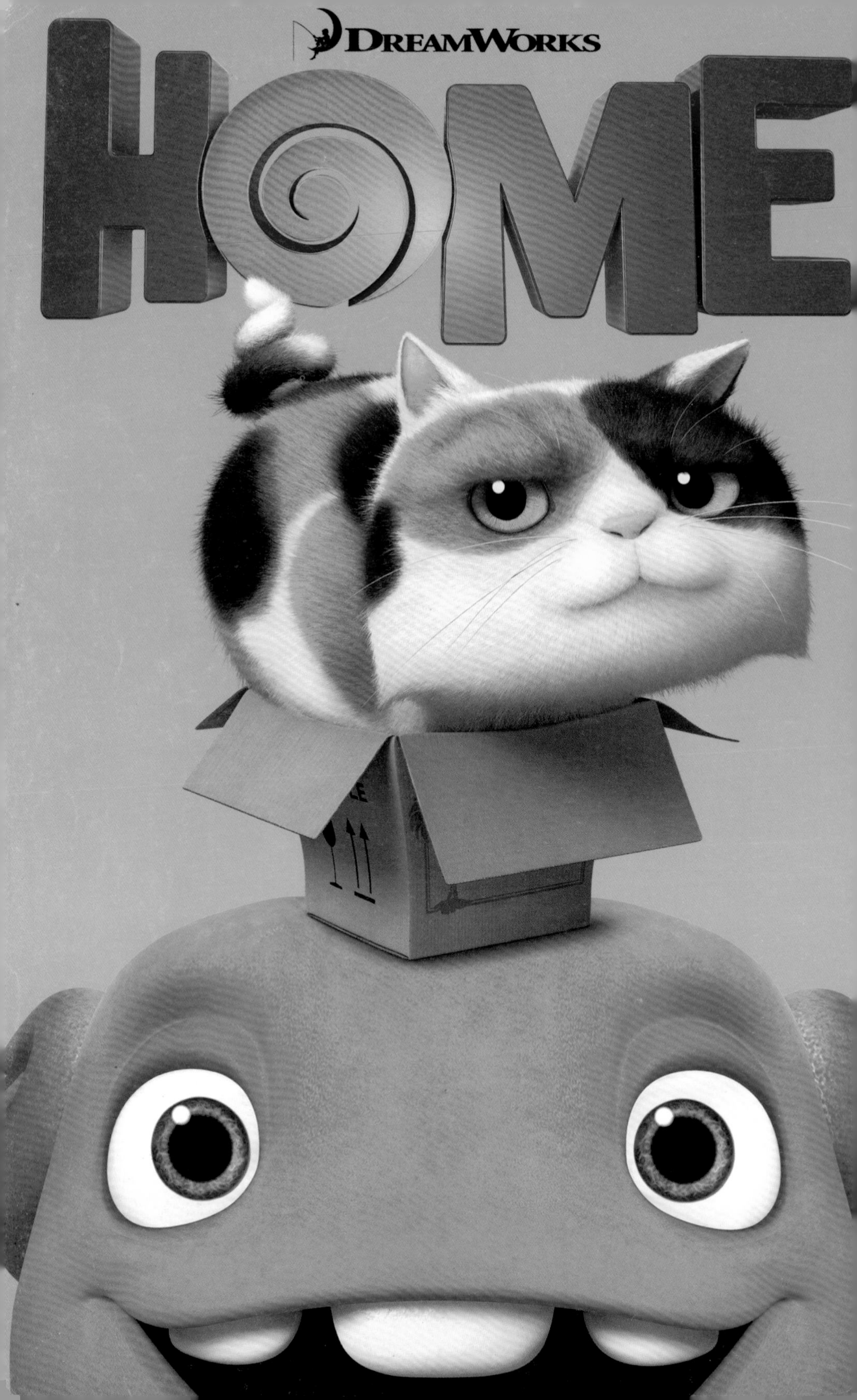
DreamWorks
HOME